"*Lost Bread* adds an essential chapter to the literature of the Holocaust. With a broad transnational sweep, it recounts a refugee's search for a new home, from country to country, until finally settling in Italy. In this elegant translation, the voice of Edith Bruck— Italy's most important witness together with Primo Levi—reaches the English reader with all its poignance and raw emotional power."

—**MICHAEL F. MOORE**, translator of *The Drowned and the Saved*, by Primo Levi, and *The Betrothed*, by Alessandro Manzoni

"Written with the emotional honesty and intimate authenticity that only a Holocaust survivor can claim, Edith Bruck's *Lost Bread* is a remarkable testimony to the author's human spirit and the blossoming of life after the Holocaust. Beginning in a small village in Hungary, Bruck tells the story of Ditke's unlikely survival through a ghetto and concentration camps before claiming and creating a new life in Israel and Italy. *Lost Bread* is a beautifully crafted, urgent novel that achieves the highest goals of Holocaust fiction: to leave the reader with more compassion and understanding for survivors of the Shoah. An unforgettable, triumphant account."

—**ANNA SALTON EISEN**, author of *Pillar of Salt: A Daughter's Life in the Shadow of the Holocaust* and *The 23rd Psalm: A Holocaust Memoir* (National Jewish Book Award Finalist)

"With every line of *Lost Bread* Edith Bruck entrusts to her readers the memories that the atrocity of the Shoah could not destroy. Memory is the salvation that defies horror. Memory keeps alive the unwavering love that a mother kneads into the bread she bakes for her children. This English translation of Bruck's forceful—yet delicate and immensely dignified—testimony preserves the intensity of the original Italian. When you slowly turn the last page of the book, you know that the tenderness and the poignancy of that *lost bread* will stay with you forever."

—**HELENA SANSON**, Professor of Italian, History of Linguistics, and Women's Studies, University of Cambridge

"*Lost Bread* is Edith Bruck's 'long poem written by life,' a minimalist fable that deftly distills the vileness of the Holocaust into heart-wrenching observations and moments that dance precariously between horror and hope. Writing in her adopted language—Italian—Bruck sheds the misery her native Hungarian tongue fated her to, allowing Bruck to find sense in survival, if not in her prior destiny. She finally speaks her name, makes peace with God, and graces our world with the gift of powerful, needful witness testimony, wielding prose honed as sharp as a diamond that cuts. A stunning addition to the Holocaust canon."

—**TARA LYNN MASIH**, author of *My Real Name Is Hanna* (National Jewish Book Award Finalist)

LOST BREAD

EDITH BRUCK

LOST BREAD

Translated by
Gabriella Romani and David Yanoff

PAUL DRY BOOKS
Philadelphia 2023

First Paul Dry Books Edition, 2023

Paul Dry Books, Inc.
Philadelphia, Pennsylvania
www.pauldrybooks.com

Lost Bread
Il pane perduto
Copyright © 2021 by Edith Bruck
Published by arrangement with The Italian Literary Agency
Translation © 2023 Paul Dry Books
Introduction © Gabriella Romani

Cover photograph: Edith Bruck with her mother, 1942

Printed in the United States of America

Library of Congress Control Number: 2023934152

ISBN-13: 978-1-58988-178-5

Contents

LOST BREAD

Introduction

Born in Hungary in 1931, Edith Bruck belongs to a small but notable cohort of writers—from Giorgio Pressburger, also Hungarian-born, to Jhumpa Lahiri, a Pulitzer-prize winning American writer—who at some point in their lives adopted the Italian language for their literary writings. In the case of Edith Bruck, the choice was as much fortuitous as intended. After being deported from Hungary in 1944 at the age of twelve and barely surviving Auschwitz with her sister—both her parents and one brother perished in the Nazi camps—Bruck arrived in Italy in 1954 as a member of a dance troupe traveling across Europe and decided to settle in Rome, the city where she has lived ever since.

During her first years in Rome, she did all sorts of jobs to earn a living, from modeling for illustrated postcards to working as the manager of an exclusive hair salon and even a stint in cinema, acting in a small role in Monicelli's 1958 iconic film *Big Deal on Madonna Street*. She did all this while learning Italian, which she used only a few years after arriving in

Italy to write her first book, *Chi ti ama così* (1959) (*Who Loves You Like This*, 2001, Paul Dry Books)—a memoir in which she recounted the horrific experiences she had just gone through; responding, like other Nazi camps survivors, to a testimonial impulse but also to a love for literature she had harbored since childhood. The Italian language, as the writer has often noted in interviews (see, for instance, my interview with her at the end of this volume), provided her with a sense of freedom from the burden of her past, as her native language, Hungarian, triggered too many painful emotions that turned into stumbling blocks in the flow of memory and testimony. But if writing in a newly acquired language was the result of her emotional response to past traumas, and necessarily the function of practical circumstances—to publish in Italy Bruck had to adopt the local language—it also denoted her strong determination to create a new home for herself by way of linguistic expression, forging a new identity as a writer. This identity, which has defined her since her first publication, is grounded on continuity as much as rupture, as her creative voice stems also from the inner child she has attempted to keep alive both during the years of captivity in Nazi camps and throughout her adulthood. As Bruck suggests towards the end of *Lost Bread*, walking barefoot as a child on the dusty streets of her village was the "most wonderful game" she has ever played—and one she has never stopped playing in her writings.

Bruck is certainly in excellent company when it comes to twentieth-century writers who chose to write in a language other than their native one—notably including Conrad, Beckett, Nabokov, and Wiesel. But the Italian literary world, steeped in the rules and figures of its canon, has traditionally been resistant to "outsiders," who are considered, perhaps, an inadequate or extraneous presence in a literary society that often harks back to its past and the glories of ancient Rome, Dante, Petrarch, and the Renaissance. As the anecdote goes, the nineteenth-century American poet laureate Henry Wadsworth Longfellow, Dante's translator for the first American edition of *Inferno*, visited Italy in 1868–69 and attended a soirée at the house of the Mayor of Florence and his wife, where he was snubbed by the Italian literati and political establishment when they realized he could not perfectly master the Italian language and fully partake in conversations. Around the same time, when Alessandro D'Ancona, a renowned Jewish Italian literary critic and philologist from Pisa, was appointed Chair of the Department of Italian Literature, some colleagues criticized his appointment because, they claimed, a Jewish person was not qualified to head an "Italian" department. What it means to be Italian is still at the center of much scholarly, political, and intellectual debate in Italy today.

In *Lost Bread*, as in previous books, Edith Bruck describes the Italy of the 1950s as a warm and welcoming country. "For the first time I felt immediately at home, after such a long, sad pilgrimage," she writes about her first impressions of Naples. Though she first observes the city with the eyes of a tourist, her view is also that of someone arriving from far away with a baggage of suffering, the need to build a new life, and the desire to put down roots in a place she could call her country. Her "country," she writes, not homeland (*patria* in Italian), adding that "in the name of 'homeland' people have committed all sorts of crimes. I would abolish the word."

As hospitable as Italy might have felt to Bruck, it is nevertheless quite notable that a young foreign woman with limited formal education (de facto terminated in Hungary at the age of twelve when she was deported to Auschwitz) would write her first book in Italian and become a well-known writer in contemporary Italy. In hindsight, her success as a foreign-born Italian writer is all the more remarkable given how few widely-known Italian writers have emerged from Italy's relatively brief, but nevertheless impactful, era of colonialism and migration. Still today, there is little equivalent in Italy of either a Salman Rushdie winning the coveted Booker Prize or a Mohamed Mbougar Sarr winning the prestigious Prix Goncourt. In 2018, however, the most prestigious Italian literary prize, *Premio Strega*, was awarded to a foreign-born Italian writer, Helena Janeczek (born in Germany, the daughter of Polish Jews who survived the Holocaust), and in 2021 Edith Bruck received the affiliated *Premio Strega Giovani* (conferred by a group of high school students, selected from all over Italy). Janeczek is one of eleven female writers (out of seventy-five awardees) who have won the *Premio Strega* since its inception in 1947; the list also includes Elsa Morante and Natalia

Ginzburg. Bruck is one of four women writers (out of eight awardees) to win the more recently established *Premio Strega Giovani* (founded in 2014). Women and minority writers are slowly forging a new literary Italy.

When Bruck appeared on the Italian literary scene in the 1950s, reviewers commonly described her as the "survived Anne Frank" (*Anne Frank: The Diary of a Young Girl* appeared in Italian translation in 1954). According to one reviewer, Edith had idealistically picked up the pen where Anne Frank had tragically dropped it after being deported and killed in Bergen-Belsen. Young and Jewish, Anne and Edith were both perceived as victims—one dead, the other living—of the Nazi's unfathomable cruelty. Today an unavoidable comparison is with Primo Levi, a close friend of Edith's, also a survivor of Auschwitz, and a writer of Holocaust literature, internationally recognized as one of the essential writers of the twentieth century. Levi's and Bruck's writing styles are notably different—the former rational and concise, the latter emotional and unvarnished—but both authors have produced, each in their own voice, some of the most eloquent pages of Holocaust narrative in the Italian language.

Not all of Edith Bruck's books are devoted to Holocaust testimony, as she has written novels thematically centered on contemporary and social issues (*Il silenzio degli amanti* [Lovers' Silence], 1997; *L'amore offeso* [Slighted Love], 2002; *Il sogno rapito* [Stolen Dream], 2014). She also wrote about her long-standing but troubled relationship with Nelo Risi, an Italian poet and her husband (*Mio splendido disastro* [My Wonderful Disaster], 1979; *La rondine sul termosifone* [The Swallow by the Heater], 2017; *Ti lascio dormire* [I'll Let You Sleep], 2019). During the latter part of his life, Bruck and Risi reunited after years of separation and she took care of him as he battled Alzheimer's disease. Overall, however, her writing career, which spans the last sixty years, is mainly based on her public persona as a Holocaust survivor and witness—an emphasis that the author has not always been happy about, as she has periodically expressed the wish to be thought of simply as a writer, rather than a Holocaust writer. Yet, with her indefatigable presence in Italian schools and universities, which she continues to visit—albeit mostly now by remote connection—and her narrative productivity, Edith Bruck, a ninety-one-year-old Holocaust survivor, shows no signs of either testimony fatigue or memory loss.

In 2021, the same year that her latest book, *Il pane perduto*, here translated in English as *Lost Bread*, was nominated for the *Premio Strega* and was awarded the *Premio Strega Giovani*, she also received the *Cavalieriato di Gran Croce*, conferred by the President of the Italian Republic, the highest-ranking honor for Italians who distinguish themselves for merit in the fields of literature, art, economic, and humanitarian activities. After decades of literary and cultural activities Bruck has reached a level of public recognition as an Italian writer that she has long deserved.

Gabriella Romani
Philadelphia, September 2022

True History
the one nobody studies
today a nuisance to most
(that made infinite mourners)
at one stroke took your childhood away

—Nelo Risi

The Barefoot Girl

Long, long ago lived a girl who, under the spring sun, with blond braids bouncing, would walk barefoot in the warm dust. On her small street in the Village of Six Houses some people greeted her, others did not. Sometimes she would sneak into the cellar where Juja was often tied and confined. People said Juja was crazy, but to the girl she didn't seem so different from other young women, and with her young heart full of sorrow she would listen to Juja's laments about her cruel family forbidding her to marry the man she loved, Elek.

Filthy though Juja was, the girl would have liked to embrace her. When, timidly, she did try to get close, Juja snatched the red ribbon from one of her braids, and before she could snatch the other, the girl ran away, worried her mother and older sister, Judit, who acted like a vice-mother, would scold her.

Her two big sisters lived in the capital, where they were apprentices with a seamstress. One of her brothers lived in a less important city. Still living at home were a rather pallid older brother and the girl, the last of six children: *grattina*, the "scrappy little girl," as they called her, a name taken from the dough her mother scraped up when making bread on the sideboard.

"Grattina be quiet!" they would say, instead of using the more familiar "Ditke" when she spoke out of turn.

Mustached farmers put their dogs on alert when she ran by. She would pose question after question to her mother, who did not have time to answer, who at most would raise her violet-blue eyes to the sky and say: "Ask Him and thank Him, for another year has passed and the wet wood no longer cries in the stove."

"And the ribbon? The ribbon?" her mother asked as if the girl had come home missing a leg.

"I lost it, just lost it," she lied, frightened to tell the truth—when her mother discovered she had been to see crazy Juja she wouldn't hesitate to give her a little smack or send her to bed without dinner. Her mother couldn't believe that this brat of a daughter she had "pooped out" into the world (yes, when exasperated she used this expression) was drawn to crazy people, to silent old men sitting on the street at the first glimpse of sun, to drooling stutterers she wanted to understand.

Her mother thought her curiosity unhealthy, but recognized she was first in her class despite the racial laws, which their town did not fully enforce. The three Jewish girls, although confined to the last row of desks, were not subjected to the laws as strictly as they would have been in the city. There they sat, beside each other: Roth the milliner's daughter, Piri; Eva, the daughter of Reisman, who sold spices; and little Ditke, the daughter of Adam Steinschreiber, a father without a trade who, for a dismal living, sold other people's animals at the market in the nearest city.

Piri was cold to Ditke because her father, who had a beard and curls—unlike Ditke's, who looked like a goy and rarely went to synagogue—thought Ditke was too poor. Eva, the twelfth child of an Orthodox father, was a good friend. But everyone was jealous the day Ditke, almost bursting with tears of joy, won the only prize for a school composition on the topic of spring. On that day she didn't walk home, she flew, waving her prize: a postcard with the image of a swallow, signed on the back by her teacher, Tarpai Klara, with the inscription, "To my best and most deserving student." Delighted, she screamed from the street, "Momma!" People opened doors, neighbors came outside; only Ditke's family seemed to have disappeared. But when she got closer, she saw her mother and sister in the sunny courtyard, removing feathers from a pillow.

"*Shhh*, what are you making all that fuss for? Can't you see? Put your hands down, be quiet! And pick up every feather you scattered with all that flapping this instant, one by one!"

"Look, look!" Ditke waved the postcard, showing the inscription while rousing a new cloud of feathers.

"That's all we needed! That you got a prize! All you do is recite poems instead of prayers," her mother grumbled—but then she looked at Ditke with soft warm eyes and a little smile that turned the sternness to a magic sweetness, infusing her face with beauty and youth.

"Would you also give me a prize, Momma? A kiss?" Ditke asked for that rare gift, usually granted only in moments of mourning, or on farewells or welcomes. When her mother went to the wedding of her second daughter, Miriam, married to a young Pole who had escaped from his country. Or when Ditke's father came back from the war as a decorated soldier, though in 1942 he was expelled from the army. Or on the death of her maternal grandmother, who in the eyes of twelve-year-old Ditke had seemed very, very old. Ditke had looked at her body, laying still on the ground, wrapped in a white sheet, until she was brought on two simple wooden planks to the cemetery, near Eva's house. Neither Piri's nor Eva's father showed up, because they were "Kohanim." Little Ditke sadly went through the names of the Jewish families in the village: Szàmeth, Grosz, Kramer, Klein, Printz, Weisz, Reisman, Roth, and Bieber, her mother's brother. Only the three members of the community who did not wear beards and sidelocks came to the funeral.

"Are they nobles, Poppa?" she asked her father.

"They are like priests. They meditate, study, they are Kohanim and have dozens of children," he murmured.

"And can't even remember their children's names," her mother chimed in.

"Don't start one of your fights," Ditke implored, grasping her mother's warm hand while trying to decipher the ritual prayer that was just starting:

May His great name be eternally blessed. May His Kingdom be established in your life and in the lives of all the people of Israel.

At the name of "Israel," her mother, dry-eyed till then, exploded with a cry that could be heard in heaven. Ditke's father held her tight, as never before, repeating her name Frida, Friduska (in Hebrew, Deborah). And in a rare, shared moment of serenity the three children clung united to their parents: Judit, the most religious; Jonas, the palest; and little Ditke. Sara, Miriam, and David rarely returned home.

After a week of ritual mourning, with help especially from Judit, Ditke's mother stood up from her seat on the floor, stiff and sore all over. But instead of walking and stretching her limbs, she stared transfixed at the grandmother's unwashed old robe. She held the robe in her trembling hands and, shaken by the sight of one of the two pockets sewn shut, called her children as if that pocket were filled with something bad, or perhaps sacred, even a secret treasure.

Wearing her glasses, she began to undo the stitches, taking out the thread, dark like the robe in which the figure of the grandmother, smaller and smaller, had become lost. At first touch the thread unraveled; all held their breath to see what was inside.

Ditke's mother, with some fear, slipped in her hand, then couldn't believe her eyes when she saw it held money. Breathing heavily, she exclaimed, "Ah, ah, ah!" The children were speechless, but when they saw there were also two golden wedding rings and a chain with a star of David, they screamed with joy while their mother, clutching the objects, began to cry. "With these" she said, raising her hand, "we will build a new house to replace this old decrepit one. Now is not the time to build, but . . . your uncle, my good brother Berti, will host us in his large house, in the neighborhood where important people live, authorities, like the judge and the teacher, Rinkó, near city hall and the police station. In a couple of months you'll have a real roof with red tiles over your head, not the rotten straw we have now."

And so it was. Ditke, Judit, their father, and a gypsy friend stomped barefoot on the mud to make the bricks.

The sun shone as it never had, clouds seemed to disperse before the scrutinizing gaze of her mother, who was cooking outside. From dawn to dusk everyone worked on the house. Ditke, for the first time, was waiting anxiously for the end of school in the summer and thought of the house as a castle, without realizing it would only consist of one large room and a kitchen, with perhaps another small room.

Occasionally a newspaper appeared in the village. Neighbor Gyula would pass it to Ditke's father who read it without showing it to his children or even his wife, as she looked on silently, with concealed alarm.

There was also a little man with a drum who brought news of the world to the village, drumming to attention an audience mainly of women dressed in black, young students, and old people. Ditke was always among them. She would listen to the man as he spoke of the glorious German and Hungarian army and the soldiers who fought in Russia, at Kursk; his tongue stumbled, his voice lost in the drumming, a wordy jumble incomprehensible to those semi-literate people. Children laughed, women crossed themselves, gray-haired men shook their heads while swearing and spitting chewed tobacco. Ditke was surprised to see she was the only Jew there. Did the others already know everything? Why did they stay at home? What were they so afraid of?

Soon the red roof gleamed, graceful green tresses of the weeping willow swayed by the window of the lone room where the three children slept in one bed, while their parents shared a small bed in the kitchen.

There was great joy in that little house. On her last day of school, Ditke swelled with pride as she returned home and gazed at the roof as if it were a compass with which to find treasure. They hadn't been unhappy to go and live with Uncle Berti while the house was being built. A few months after the death of his wife, Uncle Berti had married Jolanka, a young, beautiful widow whose teenage son, Ervin, molested Ditke. He wanted to drag her to the woods, across the dam where the Tisza river ran, to play as if he were a man and she a woman. "Woman!" her mother had yelled when Ditke anxiously ran to her with blood running down her legs. "From now on you are a woman, and you will have that thing there every month." She had pointed without naming the intimate parts, as if it were a place of shame.

It was only because of Ervin that Ditke didn't like living at her beloved Uncle Berti's house. She never confided anything, even to her sister Judit who chastised her for being vain, for looking at herself too much in the mirror. "The reflecting beauty," Judit would call her, "prissy little girl."

Uncle Berti owned a store with an inn attached. He would often sit with Ditke's father, Adam (Shalom in Hebrew), to drink a beer or a small glass of fruit brandy called *palinka*, for which Ditke's mother scolded him. "Be good, Frida," Uncle Berti, tall and well-fed, would say to his sister: "Adam does what he can. Why should a man take care of six children? Look at me, I only have a daughter and granddaughter, Erika, whom I adore, no male children and I don't complain about anything. I don't think I am better than your husband, only luckier!"

The brother's speech, one of many, softened his sister's heart, and for some time love reigned in the small house. But one day Ditke came home crying because one of her schoolmates hadn't said hello to her. Her parents were silent; at a loss for what to say to console her. Her father, typically taciturn when upset, left the house angrily, slamming the door. Her mother, left to tend the children, told her, sighing deeply, that it was nothing—a joke, such as boys do, or a bit of spitefulness. "No, no," Ditke replied, as her mother, swallowing tears and words, embraced her, as if that alone would have the effect of a magic wand. And hearing her mother say "Ditke, Ditke," her tears stopped, she forgot everything and could smile again, her heart lifted as if by a shining sun. Judit was about to say something but at a look from her mother kept quiet.

Yet, behind the silence of her father, behind the strong, sudden, enveloping love of her mother, Ditke could sense something serious was happening. She had always shunned things that might upset her— did not want to see them, hear them. She didn't care if people thought her superficial, poorly prepared to face adversities in life. She played, studied, fantasized her future as a rich happy adult who would help her parents. First, she would fix her mother's missing teeth, then cure her father's aching bones caused by war, and pay for her brother's operation—he suffered from appendicitis and the local doctor refused to come see him. At night her head filled with so many thoughts, plans, hopes. But were these only childish dreams? Would they last?

During one of the rare visits her two older sisters made from Budapest, Miriam, the married brunette who was already pregnant, brought her a real doll. Ditke was ecstatic and jumped in the air as if she had wings, so high her mother told her she could catch a bird. Sara, the blond firstborn, seemed almost ashamed of poverty. She was dissatisfied, irritable, somber, and felt less beautiful than Miriam, who was light and funny. To Ditke, they were not only beautiful, they were elegant ladies from the capital, where she too would go soon.

The first big scare came when Judit was returning from the house of always helpful Uncle Berti, who lived near her former school. On the way, she met the teacher, Rinkó, who greeted her with a sneering "Heil Hitler!" Listening to her story they were astonished—that name struck like it belonged to the devil. The white-walled kitchen seemed to darken and grow murky, as if stained by a descending cloud. Neither Ditke, Judit, nor Jonas had any idea who was behind that name. Only the parents knew, but how to convey the terror, what to say exactly? With the teacher's greeting a permanent shadow entered the family's life, a fog of the soul no words or light could lift.

Ditke's father uttered a blasphemy, spitting out, "It was not enough to have that coward, Horthy, that assassin Szàlasi!" and, as usual, left the house, slamming the door.

"May good God protect us from them," murmured her mother. "They infected even this muddy ignorant hole. The world is sick, my children. Evil has contaminated the whole of Europe. But do not be afraid, God will not throw us to these mad dogs who incite even good people to commit the most evil crimes."

"Now I understand what a group of boys was singing while I was walking on the street!" realized Ditke, who began singing:

Éljen a Szálasi meg a Hitler
üssök a zsidót a bikacsökkel

egy cini két cini
megdöglött a förabi
Bátorság éljen Szálasi*

"Stop that! Bite your tongue!" her mother screamed. Little Ditke bit her tongue till it bled, and cried out with pain, "I did not come up with it." Then her mother rinsed her mouth with vinegar to stop the bleeding, the same vinegar she'd used when Ditke hurt her knee running from the Reisman's house after Eva's father came to the door in his long, white gown and ordered her away because her father was not Orthodox. "Momma, what's happening? Why don't they want us? Aren't we also Hungarian?"

"To them, no. We are only Jews. We are Jewish. Our promised land is Palestine," she said in the tone of a fairytale. "Oh, that's our earthly paradise, waiting for us with open arms. Only there will everyone be loved. Rich, poor, old and young, as if all one big family . . ."

"And when are we going there, Momma?"

"That day will come, it will come. Don't you worry, the Red Sea will open again . . ."

"I don't believe you, I don't—you're a liar, Momma, you're not telling me the truth!"

"You are calling me a liar?! You!! The last of my children, why did I even bring you into this world?"

"I didn't ask you to. You could've spared me."

Mother and daughter eyed each other silently, regretting what was said. Ditke, who had heard those

*Great are Szàlasi and Hitler / Let's bullwhip the Jew / one two three / the Rabbi is dead / Be brave and Heil Szàlasi!

Lost Bread

21

stories about the Promised Land "waiting for us" a million times, wanted with all her heart to believe her mother. But now, even in her fertile imagination, it all seemed unreal.

"Momma, I didn't mean . . ." Ditke whispered, inching closer to her beloved mother who, raising her eyes to the sky, spoke in Yiddish to her daily interlocutor. Ditke tried to decipher the words, and in a conciliatory tone asked for the first time, who knows why, if God also spoke Yiddish?

"Of course!" her mother stated firmly, and Ditke burst into laughter mixed with tears.

"Have you gone mad?"—the girl's volatile mood-swings worried her mother; and the atmosphere overall in that new little house, with its close air and silences, became more ominous.

That summer vacation there was little playing and running with her two friends. Lenke, Endre's younger sister, brought newspapers from the city which were read only by Ditke's father and were thrown immediately in the stove when he finished. The other friend, another Lenke, who was the same age as Ditke and lived closer, would meet her less frequently. Her excuse was work. But Ditke and Judit also had to work; fieldwork such as digging potatoes and picking corn and fruit to receive some share as the landowners' generosity allowed. Even their mother would join in, though she suffered from the heat. Ditke's father had no work in the village, which was getting poorer and poorer.

Uncle Berti's inn was also having troubles. The war had decimated the local population. The elderly smoked instead of drinking; the women prayed in the large protestant church and were consoled by their compassionate pastor who himself had a wife and children. The Catholic priest came once a week to teach in the school. He was very strict and did not hesitate to punish, scolding Ditke for answering questions he asked other students. "You be quiet, it's not for you. Repeat five times: our Jesus Christ has reborn!"

"I can't," poor little Ditke muttered, terrified.

"Then get out!" Full of shame, she ran home. Unlike the time she had waved the prized postcard with the image of the swallow in her hand, now she could hardly see her way, her eyes flooded with tears.

Her mother tried to find out what had upset her, to no avail. Ditke couldn't speak, didn't want to talk about it—the name of Christ was not in any case to be pronounced at home. She would rather lie, say she'd been punished and whipped five times on her fingernails because she was talking to Eva during history class.

"It's not the end of the world. Don't despair," her mother, sister, and brother tried to comfort her. Everyone was being so kind and loving, as if they could sense the latest outbreak of contagious racism behind her tears.

The cloud looming over the house became darker and more threatening. The summer sun could not warm their souls. Flowers in the small, charming parks were dying as well, and people no longer sang the pretty popular songs in the evenings while shucking corn or pulling mint leaves from their stems in the courtyards, as they had before. The silence grew ever more ominous; only the boys still sang, but it was the song Ditke had repeated at home, for which her mother made her bite her tongue. Ditke never revealed how she sometimes replied to their singing, inverting the song's meaning: "May Szàlasi and Hitler die!" She knew her mother would worry that the boys would take revenge.

Jews were walking to the synagogue with their heads down now, keeping clandestinely close to the walls, like strangers or thieves. Sometimes youths would pull their beards or push them in ditches. At the only pump with drinkable water, they were shoved to the end of the line, and boys not infrequently spit in their buckets. All became legitimate; mimicking the grown-ups even children felt powerful.

Parents tried to hide their fear, especially from the little ones, but nevertheless it showed in their impatience and anxiety, and they forbade their children from leaving the house, or running outside. They were not allowed beyond the dam, where Ditke would gather the fruits of the forest to bring to her mother to make sauce. The woods hid edible treasures, dry sticks for the stove and wood to steal for the long icy winters. It was also a playground, with secret corners for the young and in love. And on the inner side of the dam, by the village, was a path for homemade sleds.

Everyone walked along the dam, especially on

Sundays after church, when old peasant women wearing scarves on their heads and long dark skirts trod as if following a funeral.

Ditke would ask her parents what was happening and would pose the same question: "Why? Why?" Her mother would answer with long silent sighs, while her father would say that everything would be over with the end of the war, evil would not prevail, and the Germany that had poisoned Europe would soon succumb, in fact was in agony already.

Summer went by in a heartbeat, as if it had never been. The sun grew cold, like an enemy. Fall air rushed through the broken window, smashed by a rock shot from a sling by an invisible hand.

"The glass! My God, the glass!" her mother despaired. "May God break the hand of those who did it . . ."

"Calm down, they're only boys, Frida, they're just playing. I'll have Gyula fix it. For now, I'll put up a piece of cardboard. Your maledictions are useless, like your prayers."

Then everyone tried to comfort her, all in vain; she couldn't even be consoled by Judit, her most trusted, or Jonas, her most pampered.

Ditke often met with her older schoolmate Endre, and in school she recited patriotic poems with great fervor, like everyone else; verses devoted to the Hungarian God—as if he actually existed!—and to the martyrdom of the downtrodden people. Though her countrymen saw her only as a Jew, she shed true tears for her country, where she was born and ran happily barefoot in the warm dust.

An early fall was, according to her mother, the will of God, like everything else, and it soon turned to one of the coldest winters in memory; all God's will to punish his creatures who acted against his commandments and even in his name. A world gone back to barbarism.

"Momma, Momma, stop assigning to God all the good and none of the evil. Isn't God good and bad at the same time? Momma, nothing is right here. Explain to me, please, why Piri and Eva were not in school today?"

"They can no longer go to school. But you can, thanks to your father and the war medals he earned for his country—Oh, deluded man!"

"Be nice to Poppa. I'm so happy when I get to wash his tired feet for him, his skinny back like that of a young man! Poppa is my love. Is he yours too?"

Her mother eyed her with a bittersweet smile. Ditke wanted to know everything, full of questions. Yet she was also just a child who liked to entertain herself, who would speak to her doll and tell the weeping willow not to cry, who loved anything that grew from the soil, even the smell of the earth. She was often lost in thought. Her mother took her sensitivity for weakness, and at home they called her the vain know-it-all.

No one in her family would explain why her schoolmates no longer came to class. Only the good teacher Klara Tarpai, watching Ditke stare at the empty chairs, told her, "I am sorry," with the expression of someone who couldn't do anything about it.

Christmas as well came in a rush, and the pigs' screams under the evil knives were like a siren of universal pain, unbearable to hear, an agonized alarm that rang through the village, piercing ears and breaking hearts.

There was not even the usual snow, which would coat the trees, roofs, and muddy streets an immaculate white. It was as if even the sky did not know what to do: should it weep with rain or shower light with its joyfully dancing snowflakes? Everything was gray and dark. Night and day looked alike.

"Not even the sky wants to celebrate anything," her mother whispered in bed as they all froze in fear at noises from outside, only calming when they heard a few tuneful notes.

"They are here! They came to sing like always at Christmas," Ditke cried happily, "They are my friends, listen, listen"—

For the Blessed birth of our Lord Jesus Christ
Let's sing angelic verses
For the holy day
Verses that long ago in the fields of Bethlehem
    sounded like this
Glorious ascent to all people and nations of
    good will.

"Now the wishes come!"—

"May God give us more Christmas nights that are joyous, not sad, this is our wish from the heart."

As usual, people gave money and sweets to the youngsters who sang under the windows; and for the first time her mother and father, now relieved from their fear, gave the little they had without thinking twice.

Although she did not celebrate it, Ditke loved Christmas. The trees decorated with walnuts, candies and apples wrapped in silver or gold paper, a small candle at the top adding its light to the oil lamps. The most beautiful tree was at the big house of little Lenke. Ditke would go there during the school vacation, though honestly more to see Endre than the tree.

She already imagined herself married to him—and not just as a game, like when they were younger. She was sad to realize this could never happen since Endre was Catholic and Ditke Jewish. What a shame! How many beautiful poems they could have read in bed together! They were both good in school and loved reading the same poets: Endre identifying with the poet; Ditke with the woman the poet loved—how enchanting then to gaze at each other! And Endre's father, Gyula—Uncle Gyula, she called him—with a wink, seemed to bless them.

Suddenly the Christmas silence was broken by the sound of a tambourine. The little man who brought the news, now resembling a snowman but with a voice more energetic than usual, announced that Jews could not go out after 6 p.m. and could no longer travel and leave the village. Did the adults already know?, Ditke wondered. She finally understood why many relatives, uncles and aunts, hadn't come to her grandmother's funeral.

A blanket of white silence covered the village. The few lights inside houses seemed like those of a cemetery. So much snow began to fall that doors couldn't open. Windows were frozen on the outside and everyone cried inside; wood lay damp in the stove.

"What else does God want from us?" her mother asked, sighing in the dark. "Does He want to test us?" The questions hung suspended in the smoky air.

Her father, trembling with rage, could hardly stop cursing. Her mother told Ditke, who was getting slimmer and slimmer, to climb outside through the window and fill the bucket with ice so they could have some water for the house. The village pump was completely frozen.

Gyula came with one of his fieldhands to clear the entrance to the house. Ditke was elated when the door was opened and the house illuminated by the almost blinding whiteness pouring in. The breath from the men's mouths was like a warm cloud, and before the snow could fall from their boots on the dirt floor, they had gone.

"May God bless you," her mother called to them, deeply grateful; her father shook their hands.

"You see, Momma? You see? After the bad comes the good, after the rain comes the sun, after darkness comes light, after . . ."

"Are you reciting one of your poems?"

"No, Momma. Life wrote it, not me."

"You call that life . . ."

Her father, feeling defeated, humiliated, sat at the kitchen table, head in hands.

"Poppa, Poppa," his three children cried, beginning to dance around him, trying to divert his sad thoughts.

"Adam . . ." his wife came close, and in a sweet, serene tone suggested they make a nice cup of tea with the snow.

Almost like prisoners, with the help of Uncle Berti, they reached Passover, the days of celebration of deliverance from Egypt. "Thanks to Moses, saved by water, the son of water" as her mother would say—Ditke considered it one of the most incredible stories she ever heard. "Moses was the son of Amram and Jochebed," she intoned, "and he was supposed to be killed by the order of the Pharaoh Ramses II. He was, instead, miraculously saved by the Pharaoh's daughter and raised in court as a son of the princess. When he became an adult, he left the palace to visit his enslaved brothers and decided to stay with them, even though he was mistreated by the people of God. One day, he killed the cruel Egyptian inspector who supervised the Jews' work and had to run away. He got married and had a son named Gershom, and while in the desert of Midian he saw God . . . and . . ." continued Ditke, "to Moses God revealed himself under his glorious name: 'I am who I am, Yahweh, in Hebrew *He is*, and I saw my people afflicted in Egypt and came to free them.'" Ditke related all this with a smirk, before a stern maternal look silenced her.

The sky cleared for her thirteenth spring. She took off her worn shoes and, after a long deep breath, once again went running barefoot on the warm dusty ground. This time, though, crazy Juja followed her, spat at her shoulders and harassed her with a flood of foul words.

Ditke did not mention this at home, but during the week of Passover she didn't go out. Both she and her father followed the festive rituals with unusual gravity and devotion, but without joy or song. The children even tolerated their hunger, stomachs half-empty from the absence of bread as the little matzah they had needed to last eight days.

Their good neighbor Lidi, however, gave them flour soon after Passover, which almost always fell in April. Ditke's mother's beloved hands began immediately to work the dough, punching and pushing it joyfully. During the night it would rise in the big wooden bowls, set to be cooked in the oven at dawn.

The mother was half-awake, about to get up to prepare the firewood, when there was a loud banging at the door, rousing everyone.

Before they could even ask "Who's there?" the banging repeated, more and more violently, until the door came down. Two policemen rushed in screaming orders: everyone had to be out in five minutes, with only one change of clothes, leaving money and valuables behind.

"The bread, the bread!" the mother was yelling.

"Hurry up, hurry up!" they repeated.

The father, in his underwear, kept showing them his war decorations, which they threw to the ground: "Neither you nor your medals have any value."

"Poppa, say something, do something. You know how to shoot, shoot them, fight back!" little Ditke screamed, but then she was stunned by a slap in the face. All that passed in those few minutes seemed unreal.

The mother kept talking about the bread to be cooked in the oven as she randomly threw clothes in bags and the only suitcase she owned. Ditke was looking for her doll, which somehow had ended up squashed under one of the bowls of bread dough in the confusion. Judit followed her mother's every step like a devoted shadow. Jonas was hiding behind his father, who was wandering around the house in search of nothing, still in his underwear. To Ditke, the two policemen seemed to grow larger, huge with their fat laughs, occupying the entire space of the doorway while everyone else became smaller.

"Out, out, hurry!" they kept barking, swearing.

"The bread, the bread," the mother repeated as if she wanted to say goodbye to it, defend it, even aid the loaves in their rising. Ditke was first to be pushed outside, and she was surprised to see the entire Reisman family in the courtyard with all the children, including Eva. Besides the bread, the mother was also calling for her distant children, Sara, Miriam, and David, as if they were hiding behind the broken door that the father insisted should be locked.

Reason had abandoned them and the young policemen took pleasure in watching.

Ditke exchanged a silent greeting with the Reismans, who had never felt so close. The youngest child was crying desperately in Eva's mother's arms, and in that cry Ditke recognized a pure, universal pain, an agonized scream like the pigs' cries at Christmas under the long, cruel knives. The persecutors used their common Hungarian language to inflict pain with every word and at every step as they herded the families like sheep to the small synagogue, where the other village Jews were already gathered. They implored each other silently, with eyes like frightened animals, "What's happening? What's happening?" as if their words, their questions, no longer made sense, had no more value. The only voices worth anything belonged to the policemen, who were demanding money, valuables, wedding rings, watches which only a few had. They searched men and women, checked their dress-hems, the shoulder-pads of their jackets, vilely insulting them: "Trash, rug-peddlers, skinflints, big noses pissing in your own mouths, ugly, dirty Jews get out, out of here!"

"Where, where?" one voice dared to ask.

———

"THE TRAIN, THE TRAIN! Like Endre's train!" it slipped out of my mouth, suddenly grown up, when our sad caravan of horse-drawn carts arrived at the village train station. Some villagers shed a few tears seeing us pass, and crossed themselves behind windowpanes.

"God, God, the bread, the bread!" my mother wailed while being pushed chaotically onto the train by the police and young members of the fascist Arrow Cross Party.

The families tried to stay together, and once onboard they sat on the long wooden benches with an age-old weariness. In this almost religious silence one could only hear the rhythmic sound of the train that seemed aimed at the infinite: *Ta-tam, ta-tam*—a sound that broke the nerves and accelerated the heartbeat and the crying of the baby in the arms of Eva's mother, who finally covered herself with a scarf and, overcoming modesty, quieted him with her breast.

No one had a sense of real time on the journey. Real time, like my childhood, had disappeared; as for internal time, we all had our own, according to our senses.

I wanted to be back in my mother's womb and never be born again. Judit stayed strong, Jonas had an ashen pallor, and Poppa brimmed with rage. My mother continued to invoke her other children and dwell on the five loaves of bread, by now over-risen, fallen. The devout murmured irritating prayers and a sign indicated we were at the main city of the region. The train slowed and we reached the station, where we were gathered together with all the Jews of the area.

Armed fascists, shoving and yelling, made us walk to a walled area of the city, which many of us were seeing for the first time. "The ghetto, the ghetto"—this new word began to spread among us. They opened the gate, and as families quickly huddled together, they were herded into houses already partly occupied by people from everywhere. There, atop the high wall, a huge foreign man with a booming voice, screaming in German, appeared suddenly, as if suspended in the nebulous air of an April day colder than any other. A sort of Moloch, but without the Hungarian fascist symbol of the Arrow Cross. "It's a swastika!" my father trembled.

His barking voice was easily decipherable by my parents as the language sounded like Yiddish. "Geld! Gold! Wertigkeit!"* "Schmutzige, verdamte hunden!"†

These insults hurt less than those in my native tongue, which were like stabs to the heart.

From above, the German soldier ordered two Hungarian fascists who appeared out of nowhere to start searching "those pigs"—though a few surrendered something even before being searched; especially those who looked well-off, well-dressed, without beards or yarmulkes. Perhaps they were teachers, professors, doctors. Were their lives now worth no more than any of ours? Were we becoming equal? A sense

*Money! Gold! Valuables!
†Smelly, damned dogs!

of solidarity took hold. Some donated shoes to those in need, others a coat or warm sweater, and it was beautiful. Had our common enemy, our common destiny finally united us?

Then women began fighting for the only kitchen available. Food, coming from God knows where, was as scarce as the space we were occupying. We were constantly solicited for money. Our nerves frayed, our questions increasing: How long will they keep us here? When will we return home? What will become of us?

Suddenly my brother David showed up and told us about his clandestine journey on a freight train. We were overjoyed! Now Momma was crying about her two oldest daughters, wondering where they were, what had happened to them, and where her brother Berti and her sisters could be? And what had happened to those who had lived in these semi-empty houses, with marks of removed paintings on the walls? Where, where did they end up?

Friday evening, at the beginning of Shabbat, my mother broke a candle in three pieces, lit them, and we gathered round a table for our meager meal.

Among the gossip circulating from house to house there was only one certainty: there was a beautiful synagogue in the ghetto, still open, where the next day we would all pray under an unusually warm healing sun. The synagogue rose above the houses like the Protestant church in our village. Between prayers people looked for their relatives—not finding them: Where could they be? A rumor spread that a long train with cattle-cars had left earlier from the same ghetto. The information came from a fascist who said the train had left Hungary. This piece of news seemed absurd even to my father, for once an optimist.

"We are in 1944, Russian and American soldiers are near, Nazi fascism is about over." His words were like a golden balm to a small group of people who listened as if he were a war expert and then persisted with questions: How did he know all this, from whom? Nobody had a radio and there was no little man with drums here. No newspapers. And nobody could leave the ghetto.

Germans came regularly to harass us and demand valuables, and every time they turned something up.

One day a miracle happened! "Uncle" Gyula appeared above the wall, where the German soldier usually stood. He brought sacks that came down the wall filled with God-sent goods: bread, potatoes, beans, jam, vegetables, flour, peas, and canned fruit. We couldn't believe it and began to cry with happiness, even Poppa could hardly hold back tears. I immediately asked about Endre and Lenke, then about our village, as if it were a sick person.

"And our house?"

He shook his head, hushing us with a finger to his lips. Maybe he was scared of being found out, or simply didn't want to say anything? Had he gotten here with the help of a fascist from our village? In any case he was in a great hurry to leave. Yet he left us filled with uncontainable gratitude, amazement, and hope.

"Remember this," my mother told us. "One can find goodness everywhere; there are saints and there is God. He sent us Gyula."

"A friend of mine," my father wanted to make clear, "and a man." We had never had such abundance. We shared it with the other families and were able to offer a gift to the doctor caring for Jonas' ailing belly.

For the first time, my thirteenth birthday was celebrated with a cake, although my mother was still mourning her lost bread.

It was nearing the end of May, a month I loved for the scent of the lilacs I stole from the shrubs. Instead of the Russian soldiers who, according to my father, were about to arrive, the Germans came. The ghetto was invaded by what seemed a storm of armed black crows, they barely resembled humans.

As fast as the light that fled with sunset, they pushed us from the houses, insulting us in our beautiful Hungarian language and in German, cursing our people and all our ancestors: lousy prophets, parasites, cancer. They continued the litany of abuse while surveilling the crowd, keeping us moving under the indifferent glances of a few passers-by rushing to reach their homes.

There was no time to cry or speak. People focused only on keeping pace, holding children by their trembling hands so as not to lose them, helping the elderly who stumbled as if drunk or blind. It felt like the exodus from Egypt, only without Moses, without the Eternal, and instead of the Red Sea dividing, the doors of a cattle-car opened loudly to let in the human herd with a violent push.

"Safe travels!" a Hungarian soldier yelled with a mocking smile, throwing a slop-bucket inside while extending his free arm in the fascist salute. Then he closed the sliding door and the sound of the metal bar locking in place outside shook our senses.

Piled against each other on the train with just enough space to stand, family names were called—we were together.

"Thank God, we have been lucky," my mother repeated as I clutched her so tightly that even had they cut my hand I would not have let go.

Peering through the barred windows, we tried to figure the train's direction as it proceeded with jarring jerks and jolts on the rails.

As we journeyed toward the unknown the very sight of the slop-bucket repressed our bodily needs. The only question we could think of was: "Where are they taking us? Where?" But the plea circulated mutely, like a *danse-macabre*, suspended in the vapor of our breath.

Only a week remained of my sweet May, its lovely light transmuted in our dark steaming pen. Momma began to complain of trouble breathing, and, to distract her, my adored, songful brother David asked if there was anything for him to eat. She immediately perked up and took out the little food left from what Uncle Gyula had brought us.

Our village already seemed so distant; the house where my father had tried to close the broken door was another world, gone forever, a beautiful fable of ordinary goods and bads.

At forty-eight years, Momma and Poppa were suddenly old. We children became the parents of our parents. When Momma complained of a headache my body was drawn to her, attaching like a leech.

The journey, if it can be called that, felt longer than the one from our house to the ghetto. It seemed an eternity as we huddled against each other for nights and days, with cries, prayers, fear, and shame when, under cover of coats, those who could no longer resist used the bucket.

Suddenly, with a screech of brakes the train stopped. The carts were opened and German soldiers, standing along the rails, yelled for someone to empty the shit-filled buckets; we envied those who moved first to grab the pails and go outside, following the armed soldier. Waiting impatiently for the return of the man who went from our car, we jostled each other for light, air. Someone dared ask: "Where are you taking us? Are we still in Hungary?"

"Nichts fragen! Nichts antworten!"* a young soldier responded in an almost human voice.

When the man returned with the empty bucket we could not stop asking "What did you see? What have you learned? Where are we? What did you discover?" like he was coming back from God only knew where. But he merely shook his head as, behind him, the doors all reclosed in unison.

*No questions! No answers!

From outside we could hear the barking of orders, military footsteps, and a song sang at a marching pace that we tried to decipher as the train moved on:

In meiner Heimat dort blühen die Rosen
in meiner Heimat dort blühet das Glück
Du Mädchen weine nicht, weine nicht
wenn man von Scheide spricht
gib mir deinen letzten Kuss
als Abschied Kuss. . . .*

Momma, as if taking food from her own children, gave Eva's mother and the baby a can of apricots and three small slices of bread. All that was left were pork sausages that nobody wanted—only Poppa and I would have tried them, but Momma eyed us with a deep frown; it was better to starve than bring her more sorrow.

For the first time since we had been in the train car she combed and braided my hair, adorned with the remaining red ribbon (crazy Juja had yanked off the other), dividing it in two equal parts. No one was happier than I was as I felt my mother's calm, reassuring hands on my head.

The next day Judit combed my hair. Then David, who taught me new songs he had learned in the city. David, my beautiful big brother with large velvety eyes, like my father. But no one had the violet-

---

*In my Homeland roses blossom / in my Homeland happiness blooms / You, girl, don't cry, don't cry / when the moment of parting comes / give me your last kiss / the farewell kiss. . . .

blue eyes of my mother, the most beautiful I ever saw. And my father must have adored them as well, marrying her despite the objections of his parents who, as a result, did not care much for us children. Poor grandparents and aunts, uncles, where did you all end up? Where did Momma's sisters and brothers end up?

Jonas never got a chance to comb my hair: on the fourth day, the train abruptly stopped.

11152

THE CATTLE-CART DOORS flung open suddenly, violently. We were faced with raging dogs restrained by armed men, yelling like the Moloch in the ghetto. And in the tumult of screaming, shoving, hitting, dogs barking, guards sorting—"Rechte, Linke! Rechte, Linke!"*—I lost my father, David, Jonas, and Judit. In the left line with the older women, I hung on my mother's flesh.

"Go look for your father, your father!" she begged me. I pointed to a thin man, farther away, naked among other men. "Where, where is everyone?" she continued, asking "where?" as if gone mad.

One of the soldiers came and told me to join the other line. "Right, right!" he repeated softly.

"No, no, no!" I clung even tighter to my mother's side.

"Obey, obey!" she cried while begging the soldier to leave her her last daughter. He hit her with the

*Right, Left!

rifle butt and pushed me away towards the younger women, where I found Judit.

"Judit, Judit, Judit!" I screamed wildly. "They split me from Momma, Momma, Momma!" I kept saying while they stripped my clothes, cut my braids with the ribbon, shaved my head and disinfected me. They gave me a long shapeless gray dress, wooden clogs, and a number to hang on my neck: 11152, from then on my name.

"Momma, Momma, Momma," I repeated in Birkenau, where we walked on ashes. Then in Auschwitz, where they moved us to Lager C, Barrack 11. For five weeks I kept repeating my mother's name, crying for her. Poor Judit, herself in despair, held me in her arms: "I am here Ditke, Ditke, we're together, and we'll return home together. You will find Momma again."

The block's *kapo*, Aliz, a Polish woman, sick of my crying, said, "Come, I'll show you where your mother is!"

Jumping immediately from the bunkbed I followed her to the barrack door.

"Do you see that smoke?" she pointed past the many barracks ahead of us.

"Yes . . ."

"Do you smell human flesh?"

"But . . ."

"Was your mother fat?"

"A little . . ."

"Then she became soap like mine! We've been dying for years here in our country while all of you were still celebrating Passover!"

"Um . . ."

"Did you think your dear Hungarian people wouldn't let them take you away?"

"I . . ."

"Go now, go and stop crying, your mother went to the left, right? She has been burned!"

I was speechless. Judit tried to find out what the Polish woman had said but I didn't tell her—wouldn't, couldn't—I didn't believe it, denied to myself what I'd heard. She'd probably lost her mind, her soul, living on this outpost of another world.

At dawn and sunset, soldiers with dogs came to count us in files of five, or grouped us between barracks. A man in a white gown, who said he was a doctor, pointed to some of us who then disappeared, never to return. In the latrine and common lavatory, the word spread that those women had either been selected for the brothel or were destined for scientific experiments.

Women who'd arrived before us, deported from all over Europe, warned us to remain invisible to the doctor. But how? I stayed behind Judit with my eyes closed, believing that if I could not see the doctor he wouldn't see me either. The place for news was always the latrine where we could go twice a day.

We did not work at that camp. It was an extermination camp. The daily ration of food was a fake coffee in the morning, swill for lunch—emptied of a few pieces of potato or turnip by our very barrack-mates who distributed it—and for dinner a small square of bread with a smelly cheese called *quardli*.

Everything seemed as inedible at first as, later, it was delicious. We ate secretly so nobody could grab the food from our mouths, our hands—as even mothers, daughters, and sisters did. Would we soon become like Aliz?

Hunger, lice, fear of being selected, illness, suicide against the barbed electric wire occupied our minds day and night—and days and nights felt like months, years.

I was no longer crying for my mother: I had to worry about lice, which caused epidemic typhus, about my stomach growling, about the next selection, about an abscess that could mean death, about having to pee when we couldn't go out.

Fortunately, our menstrual cycles somehow disappeared.

"I need to pee, I need to pee!" I would moan.

Judit, mothering me, suggested I go in my mess tin, which we would then somehow empty. But Marika, a thief who, though newly arrived from an area not far from our village, oversaw our room of twelve girls, saw us and, as punishment, made me kneel for five hours.

"Bitch, whore, bastard!" my sister confronted her. "You will never return home because I will kill you first with my own hands! I swear to God! Cursed animal—may you die!" Marika, a tall, plump, beautiful woman, laughed triumphantly in Judit's face, threatening her as well if she didn't keep quiet. Then she went back to the only real "room" there, which was for those lackeys who followed the Germans' orders more or less zealously and enjoyed some privileges, wielding their bit of power over us to reward and punish, for good and bad.

One day the mother of the two girls who stood next to us in line died. A sheet to wrap the dead, a candle, and a book of prayers turned up from the room where the privileged ones lived. They remained in their room while we gathered all together round the corpse on the floor and cried for that mother, the only older woman among us. Had they mistakenly overlooked her during the swift selection process on arrival? It was good Momma was not with us—but somewhere else, perhaps, with other older ones? And why did Marika and the other privileged ones stay in their room now? Were they afraid a German would come and punish them? Oh, it wasn't easy to understand the rules, the rigid discipline, the roles, or to pick up possible tricks for survival, to remain guardians of our lives without harming others in our daily struggle to reach the next day.

Judit and I deloused Eva when we discovered her in our block. She wasn't feeling well and didn't show up at the morning roll call—or maybe we just didn't see her. The block was large and crowded and we weren't free to move around.

Had three months or three years passed? Every day, hour, every minute people died: some from the selections, others during roll call, or from hunger or illness, and some like Eva, who ran and killed herself on the electric current of the barbed wire, where she remained for a long time, hanging like Christ on the cross.

That image haunted me and Judit. Eva was part of our life, our village, my far-away childhood. On that day, we promised each other not to commit suicide—for Judit had already made a few attempts to be done with her life. Then she would tell me not to worry, that she would never leave me alone, she had promised Momma to bring me back home. But when, from where? What did she know that I didn't? What wasn't I being told about that place? I had also been selected, but I managed to escape in the chaos of children crying as German soldiers put them on the truck of death.

Finally, as if we were being liberated, they moved us by train from Poland to Germany.

We arrived at a camp with thirty-two barracks called Dachau. There, too—behind a bridge, barely visible—we saw the smoke Aliz had told us about. And there, too, was a Polish *kapo*, Lola, and her friends. The difference was that we had to work, laboring until we fell under the weight of the rail-ties they made us carry. Our weakness increased with the lack of food. The Germans hounded us to work faster, laughing at our haggard faces and famished eyes as they threw sausages to their dogs.

The cold September doubled our suffering. Judit tried to help me, but how? We each had to carry our assigned weight, with only the hope our Herculean labor would end soon.

One day there was a miracle! A soldier, after finishing his meal, threw me his mess tin with the order to wash it, as I did every day. But inside the tin that day, at the bottom, he'd left me some jam—which for me meant hope, a gift of earth and heaven, strength to go forward, the will to survive and believe that at the end of darkness there would be light, that as evil brings evil, good fosters good. And, in fact, sometime later—hard as time was to measure or even consider real in such circumstances—Judit and I became part of a small group of fifteen women chosen to work in the kitchen of a castle where the officers lived with their families.

In the kitchen?! It sounded like Paradise, my mother's Promised Land—food!

We had to peel potatoes, carrots, turnips, clean the cabbage. We kept an eye on the young soldier supervising us and, at his first distraction, would gulp down some peel, shreds of carrots or cabbage leaves.

If an SS woman didn't slap me in the face for no reason every morning when I left, if we weren't kept behind at times to witness young men being hanged, their mouths open, tongues dangling, we would have considered ourselves lucky. And if, at the end of the workday, the officers' children didn't spit on us with disgusted faces.

Of course, we must have scarcely looked human— we scared them as they scared me. I wondered what they would become as adults.

And there, in that castle just a few kilometers from our camp, the second miracle happened. The cook I was peeling potatoes for asked "WHAT'S YOUR NAME?"—to me: number 11152! And, moving closer, he said that he, too, had a child, a girl like me—"like you," he kept repeating. And, taking a small comb from the pocket of his white uniform, he put it in my hand, pointing to my poor hair which was just starting to grow again. And if he was not God, who was he?

I left feeling reborn: I existed—I had a name!

One day, beyond the fence of the camp, we saw some male prisoners for the first time. They were barely alive. Although it was forbidden to go near the barbed wire, we started yelling our names, asking theirs, throwing a few stolen potatoes towards them at the risk of our lives. But they were so exhausted they lacked the strength to answer, to fight and grab for what we threw them, even to say their names. How could they have let themselves go that far?

The blessed work in the castle kitchen ended abruptly. We had to dig trenches with a spade in the frigid fall, our feet wrapped with rags inside the wooden clogs, in over-large coats distributed from a supply room where, rumor was, a child was hiding. During one of the incessant punitive roll calls we heard the most amazing news: in the crematory, which we all knew about, a German had ordered a renowned dancer to dance naked. She began the most seductive dance of her career, closer and closer to the soldier, rubbing against him until, without his noticing, she took his gun and then unloaded all the bullets into him. We applauded under the falling rain, trembling as the *kapo* of the camp, not the one from our barrack, wearing a nice tweed coat—who knows who she took that from—began to silence us with blows of a club. Soon after, a soldier came to count us.

The darkening of the sun seemed eternal, as November, the month of the dead, devoured our lives. We no longer believed the news from the latrine where people murmured about air-strikes. By whom and where?

There was no trace of Christmas. Only an enemy snow and our memories, mine and Judit's, my comfort, who warmed my hands the way my mother used to, and prayed like her too. I hadn't learned to pray because of Eva's father, who taught Hebrew to please God but would hit us with a stick on the head after each letter we read. To me he was evil and frightening like all the ultra-Orthodox, who walked fast on the road without looking anyone in the eye, who flew with their long coats as if they weren't on earth but someplace else, unknown. Yet even if I had learned to pray, I could not have pronounced God's name there. And I was also upset with Him. How could He remain indifferent in the face of such violence and cruelty?

"It's all man's fault" my mother used to say, "Where people walk there is no longer grass!"

"Then man is stronger than God?" I would ask.

"They will all pay for their actions," she assured. And who would not believe a mother?

After months, or years, after a thousand roll calls, they suddenly transferred us to Kaufering, a small concentration camp where we did not have to work.

Hunger, cold, and sickness were decimating us— and those who died beside us made us feel colder; we could not wait for them to be removed.

Bourgeois girls, the most fragile among us, were less able to fend for themselves and grew weak, like the men. The harshness of our past life gave us an edge, we resisted longer. We fought against lice, hunger—but without depriving others, as we often saw happen even between mothers and daughters. The moral education of my mother held us together even in Kaufering, where it seemed one turned on another, all against all. There was looming menace in the air, but the discipline was laxer, structure less strict. Will they kill us all—this thought tormented us—like those men in Dachau beyond the barbed wire?

Days dragged as we dragged ourselves.

Again, they suddenly moved us: to Landsberg, another small camp of the hundred subcamps in Dachau; and, according to one *kapo*, less cruel. Barely settled, we soon ended up in Bergen Belsen, where in February we were amazed to see a new group of deported women arrive with their suitcases, coats, boots, and hats. "Who are you? Where are you coming from?" Judit swore they were from Budapest. It was all as incredible as if they'd answered they were from the moon.

Soon we were moved again by train, no one knew where. When they opened the sliding door of the car, Judit fainted four times in succession. I grew desperate and screamed for her not to leave me, rubbing snow on her mouth as I shook her and, terrified, begged her to open her eyes, telling her she could not abandon me, that I would bring her home to Momma, she could not let herself die, otherwise we would die together. She came back to her senses and, dazed, could not understand what had happened or where we were.

"This is not a camp, not a camp," I told her. "They say it's called Kristianstadt. I only see a beautiful palace full of light—are we going there? No more camps, Judit. That's all finished!"

Judit stood and could not believe her eyes when she saw the palace. Was it a military base?

"It looks like the castle near Dachau!"

"*Achtung! Achtung!*" An officer in a green uniform appeared. We wondered who he was. Would we be working in the kitchen? But how?—we were too many for this palace.

"*Achtung! Achtung!*" repeated another officer walking with a soldier. They brought us to a long squat building and ordered us inside, where there were only piles of straw scattered round.

No *kapo*. Nothing. And now? we wondered, more frightened, colder. Is this the end?

Two soldiers brought in a vat of hot swill they began ladling out in our mess tins as we shoved and ferociously fought each other. "Order, you beasts! Stay in line!" they tried in vain to calm us. "More, please, more!" we implored, ogling the ladle from which swill splashed and spilled as we fought. Two more vats arrived and Judit, always first in line, was able to get another ladleful—they really couldn't tell us apart, after all, wrapped in rugs and emaciated, with eyes like ravening dogs battling for a bone.

We sniffed the air, breathing deeply, and after resting a while under the cold straw, cuddled next to each other, discovered we were not locked inside. We could go out, but where? There was no guard tower like in Auschwitz or Dachau, only that luminous palace, where we could see officers moving inside. Did they belong to the regular army? Older men without swastikas—Who were they? What were they doing there? And us? We seemed to have been abandoned. Only on the third day did young soldiers return with the vats. No bread. Only turnips, potatoes in a dense gray liquid, some flour? Whatever it was, it was hot, delicious, and spoonful by spoonful it brought us back to life.

Judit intuited there must be a cellar there, and one night she left to look for it, returning with some turnips and potatoes. We often thought of running away. But then surely the Germans would kill us, and no one would help—perhaps they even hoped we'd run away so they could shoot us. Was that why they left the barn door unlocked? Anyway, there wasn't much time to decide whether to run or not: after a brief stay at that strange place two guards ordered us to march on, who knew where?

"*Marsch! Lauffen schnell!*"* they ruthlessly hounded, as we stumbled lost in our rags, like scarecrows, emaciated and bruised, covered in frostbite.

*Let's go, fast!

"Walk! Fast! Keep going!" they kept yelling, "If you can no longer walk, tell us and we'll send you to the hospital."

With hopes of resting in a hospital bed four sisters raised their hands and the soldiers shot them.

"Understand? You walk or you die! *Ja? Marsch!*"

We understood, of course; that lesson was enough for a lifetime—if there was a life to live, if we survived, that school taught everything. By evening we arrived at a village, beautifully clean, with flowers on the balconies, wood logs perfectly stacked and covered, windows shut. The soldiers entered a farm and came out grumbling: the farmer refused their request to let us sleep in the barn. They continued cursing as they took bread and lard from their bags and told us to rummage in the trash for food. Judit saw a pig's trough but they shooed us away from that, too.

We started walking again, through small backroads populated by the "blind," as if we were invisible. A second farmer let us sleep in his barn, where we found sacks filled with grains—and to fill our growling stomachs we opened them with our teeth. When dawn came, the farmer and guards began screaming, calling us barbarians, destroyers, threatening that if we behaved like that again they'd give us no rest, we would all die on the march. We were deaf to their insults and threats, no longer caring if we lived or died. We were exhausted, indifferent—and yet at the sight of a loaf of bread someone threw us from a window we turned into tigers, fighting for a piece of that bread, which ended up mostly crumbled in the snow. The count of our dead mounted, from a gunshot, exhaustion, sickness, a farmer's "yes" or "no" to letting us rest one night in his barn.

On March 12th, Judit was turning eighteen. I, the smallest, agreed to go down through a window to the cellar of the farmhouse in search of something to eat. The girls began to yell: "Throw me something! To me! Me! Me!" attracting the attention of the guards. Judit was begging the girls to step away from the window when one of the guards came with a gun and pitchfork, swearing to smash the head of whoever was in the cellar—he'd done it before, he said emphatically, with another group of damned prisoners. My heart pounded with fear but my head remained clear: life, no matter the conditions, was stronger, more dear—I hid in a big empty barrel. The guard hit it a few times with the pitchfork, but then, failing to notice me, he left. When I no longer heard his footsteps, I slowly slipping out of the barrel and reemerged to life.

The endless march continued, seeding the earth with cadavers on the way. Windows closed as we passed, and manna no longer came even from the rare open ones. As soon as they saw us, people ran as if we were plague-ridden. We were left to feed ourselves with what we could scavenge from the trash, a few potato peels, the core and leaves of cabbage, bits of tree-bark. The guards were again eating lard and black bread. And, perhaps tiring as well of walking and shooting, they'd come up with a little game: when we reached the top of a hill and our clogs were caked with ice, they'd make us go back down and climb up again.

We'd been marching for five weeks and could hardly stand anymore. I collapsed, and Judit, along with another kind companion, dragged me on the frozen roads as if I were a sled.

We ended up back in Bergen Belsen, but in the men's camp! And—my God! It was covered with naked corpses—and some were still alive, weeping, I realized; an image etched forever on my soul.

After eating some soup in the barracks, perhaps the portions meant for those who froze to death, and after two nights of rest, they ordered us to do the worst work imaginable. They gave the few of us who'd survived the march white rags that we had to tie around the ankles of the dead before dragging them to the Todzelt, the tent of death, where there was already a human pyramid. Some, not yet dead, told us with their eyes "no, no," others murmured their names and place of origin, others managed to say: "They will not believe it, but tell them, if you survive, tell them for us, too."

Choking with tears, we nodded "Yes, yes, yes." It was already the end of March. A rumor began to spread that the liberators were bombing Germany. We didn't believe it. We'd heard the same thing in Auschwitz a year earlier. A year ago! A life ago!

"I no longer want to live. Enough, enough!" I cried, frightening Judit.

"No, no, no!" she shook me, "Do you want to give these assassins the satisfaction? Can't you feel the anxiety in the air, their disarray? Something is happening. The *kapo* asked which of us wants to go to the nearby garrison, only eight kilometers away, to brings coats to the soldiers. In exchange we'll receive a double ration of soup and bread. Come on, we'll make it. Ditke, we must go back home, yes or no?"

"Yes . . . yes . . ."

Followed by two guards, with a group of fifteen other girls, for that double ration which was life, we started for the garrison, each carrying twelve military coats. They were made of a blue nylon, soon covered with our lice. Although they didn't weigh much, after a while they felt heavy as stones.

"I can't do it anymore," I warned Judit, "I just can't."

"Wait, I beg you, the light's beginning to fade. We'll find a solution."

I groaned with the sound of the snow under our clogs. "Judit, Judit, Judit, enough!"

"Give me four of them and throw four when the guards are lighting a cigarette. Do you understand?"

"Yes, yes, yes," I wanted to scream but could not—and couldn't wait to throw the coats either. But the other girls noticed when I did, and—although Judit implored them not to imitate her little sister who was too young, too weak—they all threw some coats in the snow too, which was turning blue.

"Halt!" a guard yelled, stumbling on a pile of coats. We stopped, terrified.

"Who started this?" he asked repeatedly, in an increasingly aggressive tone. Our companions looked at us, but we all kept quiet. Then the guard took out his gun and, pointing it, said he would kill every other one of us. There was no time to guess who was going to die and I took a tiny step forward. He noticed instantly and, striding over, struck me on the head with the gun. I collapsed, bleeding, on the snow. Judit, with all her strength, started hitting the guard who, not expecting that reaction, slipped and fell while Judit ran towards me, embraced me and told me to pray with her: "Shema Yisrael, Adonai eloheinu, Adonai echad."* I began counting the steps of the guard as he approached, shaking the snow from his uniforms and boots. When he reached us, I closed my eyes, waiting for the shots.

Instead of shooting, he gave a speech: "If a shitty nothing, a dirty Jew, has the courage to raise her hands against a German, if she succeeds, well, she deserves to live. May God curse you!"—and reaching down he helped me to my feet. Yet another miracle! Judit cleaned the blood with the snow. Then we picked up all the coats, marched on, and with indescribable fatigue reached the garrison.

The young soldiers stared at us as if we were ghosts. On our way back, the guard who'd admired Judit's courage helped me to stand after each time I had to empty my bowels, for I had terrible diarrhea. Yet all I could think of was the promised bread, the double soup.

When we arrived at the camp, the guard disappeared. And we received neither the double soup nor the bread.

*"Hear O Israel, the Lord our God, the Lord is One."

New Life

WE LIVED IN agony with the dead, the cold, and the hunger, until the last roll call of April 15. The next day, though, from dawn to 9 a.m. no one came to count us. The *kapo*, who used to club us in line when some could no longer stand on their feet, was gone.

Was total abandonment death?

Judit, the hero, had a crazy idea: "I'll go out, to the Germans' kitchen," she whispered to me, and before I could dissuade her, she was running out, then bounding back in with a turnip, screaming, "There's no one there! Not even one German! The Germans are gone!"

The other girls gaped as if she were delirious. And a few minutes later we saw a jeep arriving with soldiers. Terrified, we stood to attention.

The soldiers had a different uniform, but we were scared of all uniforms. One of them approached cautiously, with an expression of shock, disbelief, disgust, and pity. He said something in English while gesturing to the rugs we were wrapped in: "Away, away!" A truck arrived and another soldier came running towards us, eyes filled with tears. Pointing to himself he exclaimed: "American Jewish, Jew, Hebrew American. You are free! Liberation! Free, free, free!"* My mother would have thought he was the Messiah. Mad with joy and tears, we screamed with the little breath we had left. We had to undress and throw our rugs in a fire. Naked and shivering, with a sense of shame I hadn't felt in front of the Germans, I blushed with a little rush of the blood that still kept me alive. Our bodies of skin and bones were coated white with DDT. We looked like ghosts. Then they gave us pink cotton dresses with little flowers and off we went on a truck to the military hospital of Bergen Belsen.

The cure began. They gave us a small amount of food, increased slowly, a little more each day. On May 3, my fourteenth birthday, I leaned out the window and an American soldier showed me a bag: "OK? Sugar, sugar. Sweet, you sweet"—from his tone I thought he was asking if I was all right. "OK," I repeated.

Judit and I did not yet dare to talk about the future. Though the future filled us, it had become a taboo.

Besides the medicines, the real cure was not having to hear—except when asleep, in our nightmares—the German language. Doctors and nurses treated us as if we were infants. And, like infants, in two months we began to grow, to speak, to walk on our feet out into the late June sun. They gave us documents with our names—our names returned to us—along with dates of birth, place of origin, deportation numbers

*In English in the original text.

and places of imprisonment. We felt reborn, free and scattered in the world of the living. And among the living I also recognized Marika, the woman who'd first punished me in Auschwitz. She came and kissed me with a violence that made my nose bleed. Before I could say a word, that vulture was gone.

"Should we denounce her or not?" Judit and I kept asking each other, and in the end we answered no. To punish would be to relive our pain. We left her judgment to God above, as our mother would have said. Momma . . . where was she? And Poppa, David, Jonas, Sara, and Miriam? We didn't dare ask too many questions, though we secretly hoped to find them soon. But when, where?

From Bergen Belsen, with our documents, they moved us to a near-by town called Celle.

A sad-looking man, tall, lanky, and thin, again recorded our names, places of origin, names of concentration camps, and detention numbers. He gave me a document I still have today.

Settled in large dorm rooms, women separated from men, the wait for repatriation began. But when?

After two months in the hospital, we began again to have presentable bodies, decent hair, and boys around our age began to woo us. Judit and I became friendly with two brothers from Transylvania. Aron, who was eighteen years old, and Miki, who was fourteen. Time seemed to have stopped there, and Aron, more than talking about the past or future, preferred to dream aloud. He and his brother were planning to steal a chicken in a nearby town. Miki made me fall in love with opera, and together we would sing arias from *Tosca* and *Traviata*. How I pined for Alfredo in *La Traviata*, as Miki longed for sweet kisses, languid caresses. Meanwhile, Judit and Aron went looking for a chicken and came back with a hen that nobody wanted to kill, but of course everyone hoped to eat. We drew straws among the dozen or so participants, aspiring guests to the most coveted banquet in the world. A boy from Budapest had to perform that thankless task, out of our sight. We then plucked the feathers, cleaned the bird and prepared the fire quickly, almost in ecstasy. Sitting in a circle, we feasted with our eyes filled with smoke on the ten small pieces of chicken as they slowly cooked. They were almost ready when, suddenly, an English soldier approached and, glaring maliciously at our treasure, booted it aside. We shouldn't steal, he said, people in town were very angry and if we did it again we'd be sent away.

I am unable to hate; I have always refused that feeling, which is toxic first and foremost to oneself. And yet I hated that English soldier who destroyed our dream and scattered it in the dust for the dogs alone to eat.

Asking for information about our repatriation at the liberators' office was useless, the answer unchanging: "Hungarians were deported last and therefore will be repatriated last."

Impatience and anxiety devoured us, as did preoccupation with the fate of our loved ones. Not knowing anything about them, waiting day in and day out for weeks and weeks became unbearable. After Aron and Miki left—not before Miki gave me my first kiss, scandalizing my sister—Judit and I decided to leave. Some Hungarian soldiers in civilian clothes, whom we had just met, begged to come with us—otherwise who knew when they'd be able to return home or where they might end up? Although they swore they were not fascist, they had no documents and must have been there illegally. "What should we do?" we again asked ourselves, "And what should we say? Should we trust them or not?" Again rejecting hate or vengeance, we relied on the hope that they would no longer be fascist if we said yes.

With a list of Jewish organizations located across Europe that would provide food to us, and to anyone in need, we began our way home without waiting for our turn to be repatriated. Disoriented in that human chaos, we moved around among soldiers and were either ignored or eyed disdainfully. Everywhere, people tended to reject us. They were in a rush, fearful, unnerved, suspicious, and wanted to be rid of us as soon as possible. At the Bergen Belsen station—the same station where we'd carried military coats to the young Nazi soldiers who'd eyed us as if we were ghosts, where my life had been saved once again—we boarded a freight train full of coal headed to Pilsen in Bohemia.

From there, dispersed in the world of the living with our useful clandestine friends, those Hungarian ex-soldiers who could orient themselves better than we could, we reached Bratislava, feeling nervous. The city was once Hungarian and familiar to us. A sister of my mother, named Honei, had lived here.

At the assistance center we received food rations that, as usual, were abundant for two—an abundance we welcomed in our eternal hunger. And we shared what we had with our two hungry friends. Despite the doubts we'd about them, men of few words and possibly false names, sharing food with them became a ritual, and walking on the dreamed-of ground of Bratislava made us feel truly free. Being there was an incredible experience, and we almost didn't realize when our friends slipped away, barely heard them say, "God bless you! God bless you!"

By makeshift means, we reached Budapest. We stood at the station holding our sacks while passersby jostled us and brushed by with dark, indifferent eyes. Only a group of soldiers seemed in a happy mood: they sang in Russian with a triumphal air and wore hats with a red star.

Since we were no longer seeing German soldiers or the Arrow Cross nationalists, we instinctively smiled at them as they came toward us, bottles of vodka in hand. I kept smiling as I recognized the song from Dachau, where I'd heard some Russian prisoners sing it. A man walking by warned us in Hungarian to be careful, whispering disdainfully that "those ones there rape young and old women, all of them." Judit pulled at me, but I protested: "Don't pull me! Don't pull me! Do you know what they're singing?"

"No, but let's go, let's go!" She pushed me away as I sang too:

Devushka, devushka
Kak tebya zovut?
Idi syuda
Davai pizda
Yëb tvoyu mat'!*

"Shame on you! How can you even say those filthy words? If Momma heard, she'd kill you!"

"It wasn't me who came up with it."

We kept running, short of breath, and saw the city; gray, gravely wounded, covered everywhere in debris, in total ruin, not only physical but human as well: stores empty, people trudging with heads down, filled with sadness, their bodies shrunken, faces dark. Only Russian soldiers moved about freely, often drunkenly, on foot or by car with a victorious air, dominating the area as the Arrow Cross nationalists had, before.

Judit was still in a mood to fight with me, because of the song or, perhaps, simply from anxiety, fear that no one we hoped to find would be there.

We immediately visited the center for assistance, where a man who neither introduced himself nor asked us anything gave us one thousand five hundred *pengő*, with a receipt, clarifying that the money was all we would get and was meant to get us to our village—and have a good trip.

*Girl Girl / What's your name? / Come here / Come on cunt / Fuck your mother!

The address of our sister, Miriam, who lived in Budapest, resounded in our hearts until I thought mine would explode. Arriving at the courtyard, we noticed several small balconies, onto one of which a woman came to beat a carpet. We asked if she knew Mrs. Rottenberg, but she didn't reply. Was she pretending not to hear us? Did we frighten her? Did she hate Jews? But it was a Jewish area! Our confusion soon evaporated into pure joy: Miriam appeared on another balcony with a baby in her arms.

"Tomika," she said, pointing to the boy, and adding: "I'm already a widow. My husband froze to death while marching towards the camps, after years of forced labor." She could only feed us for a few days, Miriam continued, because everything was rationed, or sold on the black market. We were still standing at the entrance, agitated, and she was almost defensive in the face of our hugs and the cries that choked us.

"The baby, the baby, you're scaring him," she admonished, shaking free of our arms. "Enough crying and talking! Let's go!" Once inside we basically filled the tiny apartment, and with a few words Miriam made explicit that there was no room for us there. We could go to Miskolc, she said, to Sara, who was married to a well-off man, and our brother David was already there. He survived—our father did not.

"Go and wash yourselves. I'll look for something clean for you to wear before you get close to the baby. I'll fix you something to eat. There's plenty of time to talk about what happened. Here as well we suffered terribly, the hunger, the terror: the Danube was red with the blood of those shot by fascists. And the ghetto. Oh, I could tell you, I could tell you . . ."

Then she began talking distractedly about a Spanish diplomat who saved hundreds of Jews in Budapest. Only later did I discover that this "Spanish diplomat" was in fact an Italian businessman from Padua named Giorgio Perlasca. When I met that blessed man in the 1980s, he was tall, thin, and humble, with flashes of sweetness on his face and resolve in his eyes. I wondered: "What am I supposed to say to him? Thank you?" What could be said to an ex-fascist who did something incredible during the darkest times in Nazi-allied Hungary? That he was an ordinary man who could no longer stand the massacre of his fellow humans? It was a stirring of his soul that inspired the idea of passing himself off as the General Consul of Spain, which allowed him, at the risk of his own life, to save thousands of innocents destined to annihilation for purely racial reasons. Around the same time, the actual Swedish diplomat Raoul Wallenberg did something similar in Budapest. But he was imprisoned on the arrival of the Soviet army, and his luminous life, at only thirty-two years of age, was snuffed out in a thicket of darkness that remains obscure to this day.

Back then we completely ignored the stories of these two righteous men. When Miriam told us about them, we wanted only to interrupt, run away—but to where? We felt we were a burden even to ourselves. We wondered if life had hardened our sister. She used to always be happy, light, full of vitality, even frivolous, attractive, courted. She seemed changed, more dismissive than welcoming. Seeing this, our hearts shrunk.

"Is it true that Russian soldiers rape women?" we asked, just to say something.

"Yes, be careful."

"And David? How is he? What did he say about Poppa?"

"You can ask him all your questions. Now get washed. We don't have anything worth remembering, no good stories to tell. The only really nice thing is seeing you alive. But what kind of life awaits you?"

"Life," we repeated in chorus.

The city we'd dreamed of a thousand times was colored only by the Russian flag, with signs of battle everywhere.

The blue Danube soon digested the blood of the dead, turning yellow like the star worn by the executed. The early autumn gray cloaked everything. No smile could be seen except on the Russians. Who knows why Momma had been waiting for them . . . Judit and I exchanged glances in a silent dialogue, as if to say that there was an abyss between us and those who had not experienced what we had. We felt we belonged to another species. What was happening? We'd thought the world would be there to welcome us, kneel in front of us; but now what was left of our life seemed a weight. Whether this was real or imagined, during the brief time we spent with Miriam we were unhappy. Her economic situation was unstable, the house miniscule, and we weren't even free to speak, because she'd stop us. Because of her child?

Self-defense? It wasn't easy for Judit and I to get her to stop talking and crying.

Disappointed but hopeful, we left for Sara's house—to see David too. We took a train, locking ourselves safely in our compartment for the ride. Then, with Sara's address in hand, we found the beautiful villa and knocked loudly, more and more emotional at the thought of being reunited with our brother.

A woman dressed in black opened the door, and after eyeing us as if we were beggars, called, "Lady Sara, Lady Sara, are these perhaps your sisters?"

Lady Sara stood on the patio, blond, beautiful in a rust-colored maternity dress and two glistening gold bracelets; unmoving—only her blue eyes descended blankly, as if she didn't recognize us.

"Sara, Sara!" Judit called, but instead of giving us a welcoming hug, Sara told her maid to immediately prepare a basin of hot water in the courtyard for us to wash.

"But we've come from Miriam's house, we don't have lice, we're clean. Where's David? Where is he?"

"He's at work, with my husband."

"Well, call him!" Judit protested, "Miriam said you knew we were coming."

"Don't be silly! I'm expecting a baby and need to stay calm. Come, come here for a kiss, but first wash yourself."

Would it have been better to die than to kiss her? we silently asked ourselves. What had happened to her? Sara had always been serious and cold, always wished she'd been born in a rich family, but to be welcomed like this. . . . We were in despair and again wanted to run away, but where?

"To what world did we return? Why did we fight so much for survival? Why, why? David, David!" we invoked, hoping to receive a true embrace from him, an understanding that would not need words.

Sara, probably feeling a little guilty, asked us to be patient and eat some food that Maria, the maid, was going to serve us. Soon we would see David, she said, with the rather severe expression that, when we were little, made us call her "bundle of rage."

Finally, David arrived, our beloved brother who was now twenty years old. After a long, sobbing embrace, our tears melding together, he told us once and for all the dreaded truth: that he'd been with our father, and one day when he returned from a work detail, Poppa was no longer in his bed among the terminally ill. He'd had to look for him in the Todzelt and, rummaging there, he'd found him, wrapped him in his only blanket, and murmured a prayer with the little breath he had left. David himself barely survived, by a miracle, and thanks to one of our cousins. . . . He promised to tell us more later.

Desire to talk swelled inside us—and, unlike Judit, I swelled with more than words. Soon my weight doubled, from about 90 to nearly 180 pounds. They said it was because I was still missing my monthly cycle, blocked by something from my time at the camps; that it would soon come back and then I would no longer be bloated.

Soon Sara's husband arrived, smiling. He looked like a pleasant man, spoke in a strange dialect, and welcomed us much more warmly than our sister had. He immediately gave me a nickname, Munzi, at which my sister made a face. Later he would make jokes about Jews, about the muddy hole we used to live in and how he made a lady of our sister. He also warned us that in the country even fascists pretended to be communists.

After a short stay at Sara's, feeling ever more uncomfortable with the situation, we decided to visit our village, without David who worked with his brother-in-law in a paint factory. By that point, we'd learned that our mother and our brother Jonas would never come back.

When we arrived at our village, overwhelmed with emotion, people looked at us as if we were their enemies. They seemed stunned, incredulous, perhaps even frightened we'd take revenge or report them. Our neighbors defensively said, "I never harmed you and never took anything. I was not evil, Jews brought communists, the new bosses. I gave a loan to your father. I kept the millet your mother gave me to look after. I kept the duck. I . . ."

"The house, our house!" We ran to see it and found it emptied out, broken into, some pillows strewn round and soiled with shit, Momma's Singer sewing machine smashed. At the back of the courtyard, in the manure spilling out of the nearby barn, we found some family pictures, which we took. Overcome with exhaustion, in indescribable pain, we turned our backs, never to return, without meeting even those we remembered fondly: Uncle Gyula, his son Endre, his daughter Lenke, and Lidi, the neighbor. Why hadn't David warned us about the state of our house and dissuaded us from going to see it? We felt ever more alone and abandoned.

Miriam was about to get married again, to one of our cousins, who had lost his wife and two children; soon afterwards they moved to Czechoslovakia. Judit decided to go to Budapest to join a Zionist group in the hope of reaching Palestine; she would live our mother's dream in her place.

"Come with me," she insisted—for a long time she tried to convince me. "There is no place for us here, what do you want to do?"

"To write."

"Write what? What are you thinking? Who would you write to?"

"To myself."

"We will learn a trade, the language of our ancestors. We will be at home, the Promised Land, the land God promised to Moses."

"I've already heard this fable."

"We can't leave each other: you and I are one, reborn together."

"No, we are two. I'm studying piano at Sara's house, and I've started to write. I'm beginning to lose the bloating."

"Obey me! You're still a snotty child. You like it so much at Sara's?"

"I don't like it anywhere, but I no longer obey anyone either."

"Are you waiting for Sara, who's a nervous wreck, to kick you out of the house? You'll end up on the street."

"Then I'll live on the street."

"And what will you do, whore?"

"If there's nothing better . . ."

"I saved you, but I can kill you, too!"

"I delivered myself during a year of labor. Let's not fight, but I won't sleep in dorms again."

"And how do you know you would sleep in a dorm?"

"I can't stand crowds; I always need to see a way out."

"Then you'll leave me alone for a piano? You can write anywhere."

"I don't know Hebrew like you. I can only write in Hungarian."

"You will learn."

"When? I need to write now."

"To lose weight?"

"I need it to breathe."

"Don't be your usual know-it-all self. Use your head, be normal for once."

"I am."

"So you'll make me go alone?"

She cried a lot, and I felt more orphaned than ever. Yet, despite the sadness and guilt, I resisted.

"Uncle Moriz is in Palestine! Don't you remember him? But you were just born when he left. Momma spoke of him like a saint."

"But we never heard from him, he never got in touch with us. Wasn't he a baker?"

"How can you remember all this?"

"How can one not remember?"

"I had a good memory in school too, not just you. Please, I am begging you, we can no longer live here. They don't know what to do with us."

"And do we know how and where to live?"

"In Palestine."

"Who lives in Palestine now? The English—those who destroyed our chicken in Celle! That was really cruel. American soldiers were more human."

"And if Sara continues to scorn you with her icy blue eyes?"

"I'll go stay with David."

"But he just got married and they live in a single room—the other's occupied by an invalid tenant they're letting stay there. I am not going to leave you alone."

"I will join you soon. And you'll let me know if the Promised Land really exists."

"How can you not believe that? How can you doubt the word of our mother and of God?" She gave me a fiery look. "For this we survived?"

"I don't know. Let's live—we'll see by living. Our real sisters and brothers are those from the camps. Others can't understand us. They think that our hunger, our suffering is the same as theirs. They don't want to listen to us. This is why I'll speak to the paper."

"And you think you're normal?"

"Yes, the paper listens to everything. Go in good health and in lucky times, as they say in Yiddish, and for now write to me at Sara's."

Seeing her go, I felt like I'd been left in the middle of the desert, without the voice of the Eternal.

Sara's heart remained cold as winter. I kept losing weight. I was writing but hiding it. My clothes were threadbare, something that roused compassion from neighbors who made me gloves and a wool scarf.

One day my brother-in-law, who traded salt with Romania, left with my sister on a business trip and I stayed alone in the house where the butter was under lock-and-key, inaccessible—Maria, the maid, checked on me as if I were a thief. An old spinster who was supposed to give me piano lessons gossiped and insisted I play scales, while I wanted only to freely play my mother's and father's songs. And once, when I did, she closed the piano, squashing my fingers on the keys and almost breaking them, triggering memories of other violence I'd suffered—and woe to those who would raise a hand like that to me now! She apologized profusely, the poor thing. She had no idea of my problems.

During my sister's and brother-in-law's absence a Jewish doctor showed up from a nearby town, saying he was their friend and would be sleeping there, as he usually did.

As soon as I went to bed he assaulted me, and I reacted furiously, fighting him off. He even got offended! In his mind, I was a poor stupid country girl and he thought it was his right, assigned by social standing, to make me his prey.

Then, like a coward, he begged me to keep silent about what had happened.

But Maria, the maid, had been spying on us and told my sister who knows what when she returned. As if Sara had just been waiting for an excuse to seize on, she slapped me, called me a whore, and sent me away.

I wouldn't see her again for twenty years. I went to stay with David, in his wife's town. He listened to me, perplexed and mute. I shared the young couple's single room, partitioned by a sheet. At night I could hear them making love. During the day, Ivan, the tenant who was in a wheelchair, played the guitar while I sang along to his sad tunes. Some afternoons, at the bottom of the garden where it sloped towards the river Bodrog, I wrote, and read books Ivan leant me: novels, poems . . . I liked them all.

I devoured each line, every page, volume after volume. At sunset, which I loved, I wrote with a pencil in my notebook. I had already attracted several suitors and received my second kiss, from a good-looking middle-class boy. My brother was worried: he thought a boy like that, from a well-to-do family would never marry me. He feared I would give in to him.

"Feri likes you, too," he made sure to tell me.

"Feri who? Rozenthal? Poppa's friend? He could be my father!"

"He wants to get engaged."

"I don't."

"Let's agree to the engagement and you'll settle with a serious man. I already made arrangements with him. I'm doing this for you. You'll be protected, and I'll stop worrying. Listen to me. We may decide to leave this town any moment."

With a heavy heart and trembling legs, I consented to the engagement, though without allowing any kissing.

I would ask Feri questions about my father, what he was like when they'd meet and drink together, away from us. I was searching for something to make me better understand my father, so taciturn with my mother—a source of many fights between them.

Unfortunately, he had nothing to reveal about my father, and nothing else to give me. Soon he left for Canada, where, I learned later, he married a distant cousin of ours. David became a member of a group of "new" communists and was getting ready, secretly, to leave Hungary. First, though, he was organizing my escape to Slovakia to stay with one of his brothers from the camps. In the meantime, after selling his wife's house, he bought some jewelry, which people were selling to buy food, since it was so scarce then. He gave it to me to safeguard and take away.

On New Year's Eve of 1946 I was beyond the Hungarian border, in Bratislava. A young man was waiting for me. He spoke Hungarian quite well, though with an accent and grammatical errors, and he welcomed me with a hug. The house where I went to stay was large and nearly empty, apart from beds. Alex, David's comrade from the camps, had a wife who lived there too, but otherwise the house was filled with a constant stream of people who were lost, like me, not knowing what to do with their lives, how to start living again. People who couldn't find ease either in themselves or with others, who were in some way broken, whose lives had changed forever.

I waited in vain for my brother in that kind of commune, which, in time, I learned was financed by Jewish agencies with the goal of sending us all to Palestine. In fact, a few times a young, robust, blond man, "the new Jewish man," visited and, in a jumble of languages, explained that we would all soon leave for our land, where a clandestine war was taking place against the occupying English and Arabs. Shortly, we'd be transferred to a transit camp in Germany, on the outskirts of Munich, and trained with military drills. Finally he added: "Be brave! No complaints and no *oy vey oy vey* in Yiddish!"

I felt like crying and I wanted to join Judit. But where? I asked an agent who had just arrived from Palestine and gave him information about Judit. He told me that the ship on which she'd been traveling to "the land of our dreams" had been confiscated by the English, the migrants taken to Cyprus.

David moved to the city where Sara also lived. His wife was expecting a baby. The jewels he'd given me for safekeeping had been stolen—how, when, and by whom, I had no idea. Feeling lonely and left to my own devices in that transient and promiscuous life, I fell in love with a man who was eating me up with his eyes, smiles, a shade of cynicism and deceit on his voracious lips—a man who knew women liked him and often didn't return to our communal home at night. Why had I chosen a man like him, who took my virginity with a gesture resembling the kosher killing of a chicken, its throat opened with one sharp cut before being thrown bleeding in the courtyard of the synagogue! Was he disgusted by the blood? Why such violence without a caress? Was he punishing women through me or was I punishing myself? Why did I allow it? Was I throwing myself away? I wanted to be done with my useless life, my youth in such a brutish world. I only had my sixteen years, until then defended with all my strength, and now I despised myself. Or did I love him? Was I ill? Maybe I simply wanted love. Here was someone for whom I existed, who desired me even though he had other women, taking his pleasure with no thought of mine. Why? Why?

Some time later we met and exchanged brief greetings in the transit camp outside Munich, where people came to the fence around our perimeter with empty pots, asking for food. I gave them all that I could.

More months of waiting, filled with Jewish songs, marching, military steps, speeches about our ancient land that animated all of us: survivors. I was fascinated by the songs, which were beautiful, like the ones sung by the communists in the little town where David stayed. Who doesn't like such words as democracy, social justice, equality, bread for all, land to the oppressed, exploited, or enslaved, culture and consciousness to the people, the workers, eradication forever of fascism, of the power of the rich and the Churches, *etcetera*. Sweep away the nobility, the bourgeoisie which feeds off people's blood . . . Chin up, people, hurray for the proletariat! The words of the instructors-agents-warriors did not resemble my mother's fables, whose sweetness I could still taste in my mouth. Their voices were rough, bitter, new, different from ours. They seemed another species: sure of themselves and their new words as they stood before us, helpless martyrs of the ghetto and the camps, hungry for love and peace.

"It was born! It was born! The Russians were the first to sign! The radio, the radio. Let's listen! Ben Gurion is speaking. Pay attention, here is the anthem, the national anthem! The *Hatikvah*!" Even though we did not quite understand its meaning, the anthem resounded in our hearts, and tears flowed down our cheeks. It kept playing on the truck that brought us to France, to Marseille, where for the first time I saw the sea! There, in mid-summer, we were gathered in yet another camp, waiting impatiently to be transferred to the newborn Israel where I would finally see Judit, and possibly my father's brother. Sad, that my mother's dream was never realized, but for us it became an impossible reality, made of pure emotions and biblical nostalgia.

Noah's ark arrived in September in the port of Marseille. We settled in the cargo hold, among a diverse multitude, people of different ethnicities and unfamiliar customs. People of color with long beards and coats walked barefoot and chewed roots, mumbling and spitting green saliva.

"Who are they?" I asked loudly, feeling my own strangeness as well, feeling again like an unknown from another world. I brimmed with wonder, sitting in the old ship that swayed like Moses' cradle on the Nile, drifting towards the infant State.

A voice behind me said, "They are Black Ethiopians and Moroccans." Turning around, I saw a tall young man with a slightly crooked smile and olive skin. I had noticed him earlier when, running breathlessly, he was the last to board the ship. Extending his arm, he shook my hand firmly and, speaking Hungarian with a wry grin, said his name: "I am Braun Gabi from Budapest, and you?"

"I am Ditke, from a village you wouldn't know."

"Are you alone?"

"No."

"Who are you with?"

"My brother and sister."

"Where are they? Here on the ferry?"

"In Israel."

"Then you are alone here, right? I had so much fun in Paris."

"What were you doing there?"

"Having a good life!"

"Alone?"

"There is no lack of beautiful women in France, but not like you."

"The ship is rocking too much, I'm getting nauseous."

"Do you get seasick? I don't. I'm going to be a sailor."

"I'm feeling sick."

"Let's go up, you can vomit in the sea." He took me on deck, and during the next nine days and ten nights, between spells of vomiting, I fell in love with his hands, which held my forehead the way I used to hold Momma's when she threw up.

He even came with me to the bathroom when my stomach ached. His face would only turn grim when I didn't allow him to explore my body. I was in such pain the entire voyage that when we arrived I could hardly stand on my feet.

Reality

AFTER SINGING the Israeli anthem in total chaos, with people stumbling against me, pushing me around, I wanted only to find a bathroom on land, and I finally saw the sign "WC" under my feet. In the meantime, my boyfriend was gone; I barely noticed him getting on a truck going who knows where.

I got in line to be registered. Men and women, according to age, were being enlisted in the army and I, still seventeen, was transferred to a camp in the desert: prefabricated houses with tin roofs, built on sand.

Where am I?, I called at night, amid the howls of wild dogs: Momma, Momma, where am I?

And what of the reality I'd been afraid of finding when I refused to accompany Judit?—and where was Judit, where? A dream evaporated, gone with my mother: her waiting for the Russians, my father for Socialism.

Behind me, a *tabula rasa*. In front, people lined up with bowls for food, and an energetic woman named Ruth who kept order, especially among the most impatient, under the searing heat of the Middle East sun.

Language among us was mixed, Babelic. We were from all over and were settled according to where we came from. Hungarians with Hungarians, Romanians with Romanians—while in our countries we had only been Jews. In the camp office I learned that Judit and David were already in Israel. With surprising speed, they informed me that my brother and his wife and small child lived in an agricultural cooperative, and the child took my father's Hebrew name, Shalom. Judit lived in a neighborhood on the outskirts of Haifa with a man she'd married in Cyprus, and they had a baby named Haim, "Life." Our Uncle Joel was in Tel Aviv with his two boys, Avi and Itai.

But without money how could I go to see them? I asked myself this every day, until I heard that everyone moved around by hitchhiking. Private cars were rare, and my first rides were on military jeeps and trucks as I explained where I was headed, Judit's address in hand.

Her small house stood on sunken terrain. It had a large terrace where I saw a carriage with a baby. A tiny baby, a marvel! A cute beaming face and two sparkling dark eyes.

I leaned down to kiss him, covering him with tears which made him cry and made my sister run out in her apron and slippers, almost fainting when she saw me.

"God, God!" she rejoiced, scolding me at the same time for not having come with her to begin with.

She began telling me about herself, and I told her about me—keeping quiet about the man in Slovakia, though I did say something about the boy from the ship.

"What will you do now? Will you move in with us, or with David who arrived three months ago? Single people do not get assigned lodging. Life is hard, but here we are at home—the home of the Arabs, who want to throw us in the sea. For lack of better options, my husband is working as a traffic cop. He isn't happy. He wanted to be a painter, like you want to be a writer. Are you still writing?"

"More than ever. The words I want to express grow and grow—if they were conceived children I'd deliver them, as many as those who were annihilated."

"I don't understand you and never will. What are you saying? Study Hebrew, learn a trade. Here, let's go inside my poor house, two little rooms and a kitchen. The terrace is large and is good for the baby but obstructs my view. Haifa is beautiful, you must see Mount Carmel."

"I want to see David. Have you already seen Uncle Joel? Does he look like Poppa?"

"I rushed to see him when I was pregnant. He has nothing of Poppa. His wife, a heavily made-up Polish woman, put a cup of coffee with milk in front of me without sugar; there is scarcity here, too. The country is still not a country; it's just born—young like him, my baby. Our uncle is quiet like our aunts—poor things, all gone. There's not a single Jew left from our village. But let's talk about other things. My husband is handsome, but younger than me, and he doesn't like me to wear shoes with heels. Today he'll be late, he has the afternoon shift. Should we eat something? Should I make you the cake with cheese that Momma used to make? Do you remember that German who wanted to kill you? And do you know who I met here? Aliz, that vulture, our *kapo* in Auschwitz. Should we report her? And guess who else I met? Marika, the other vulture! And good Terez who helped me drag you to the end of the march."

"The baby's crying."

"He already knows everything. I told him he has neither a grandfather nor a grandmother."

"You shouldn't have done that! I want to return to Pardes Hanna before nightfall. I have to go, I need to go now." I wanted to escape those stories, our memories.

"I can't let you go!"

"I'll come back soon."

"Why all this rush? Who's waiting for you? What are you up to? Are you flirting with someone?"

"No, I just need to go. Tomorrow I'll go see David and then Uncle Joel. I want to see them."

"You didn't tell me your first impression when you stepped on our land. I kissed it."

"I was very sick on the ship. I vomited the whole time, and when I landed I was shocked to see the toilet paper in the port bathroom with Hebrew writing."

"They were newspapers, silly! Are you happy we're all here?"

"I don't know . . . from Momma's mouth the fable was more enchanting."

"Are you saying you're disappointed because of our mother? Come on, eat."

"No, no . . . Perhaps it's my fault, I can't seem to be happy anywhere. I don't like the world and can't change it."

"I wish you could change it, but I'm afraid it is the world that will change you."

"You named your child Haim, 'Life.' It's a beautiful name."

"Yes, we must replace those who . . ."

"Yes, yes, I got it. That's enough, now I have to go."

"Here's my husband, Amos."

Lost in his uniform, he had a pensive expression, as if something troubled him. He stepped timidly towards me, then almost shrank when I tried to greet him with a kiss.

"You two don't look alike."

"Are you saying she's more beautiful than me?" Judit asked him.

"No, no."

"Since she was young she's spent hours in front of the mirror thinking she was the fairest of all," added Judit, who was anything but ugly, only somewhat insecure, serious, argumentative, a little like Momma.

Before she could reminiscence further about my childhood and our death-filled past, I ardently kissed the baby, "Life," then also kissed Judit, who was more than a sister to me, and the introverted Amos, with his beautiful face and armored heart.

I left the house feeling more lost than ever, my legs trembling as if I were drunk, confused. On the road, I raised my thumb and stopped a van, driven by a military man who looked trustworthy. I mentioned the name of the camp and he answered, "OK."

"My name is Ditke," I said in Hebrew, and from my accent he immediately understood I was Hungarian. Mixing four languages together he was able to convey that he'd lost a brother in the war; that we were surrounded by enemies, they were at our door; and that even we, the newly arrived, had the responsibility to defend our land.

"Why aren't you in the army? Soldier, soldier?"

"Oh no, I'm not of age. And I don't want to wear a uniform, to kill or die. I come from Auschwitz."

"Auschwitz, Auschwitz. Enough! You must be strong, you must live and die with dignity."

"I want to get off," I said at the center of the city.

"OK, OK, OK!"

Then he seemed to change his mind and got off with me, saying: "Let's go to the Café Nizza chez Ungar. Magyar, Magyar, I'll offer you a sacher torte."

The robust man behind the counter had a familiar face. He reminded me of Uncle Berti, who was gone, and I teared up thinking about our best-loved uncle. Turning my eyes from him, I looked toward the glass door at the entrance and saw, appearing like a ghost, Gabi, the young man from the ship. I ran and hugged him as if he were Jonas, my lost, pale little brother. He also hugged me, like a lover, and was immediately jealous of the soldier who'd given me a ride and who now, with a rudely grunted "OK" and "shalom," left me there with my sailor. I began telling Gabi about me, Judit, David. He didn't have anyone. He was an only child, loved engines, and worked as a mechanic on a military ship. His salary was meager, and, he added jokingly, it would be convenient for us to get married; obviously the army would cover the cost, and we could even obtain lodging and a family check. Listening to him made me dizzy, and he swore that he loved me. I feared—and yet, not too much—that I'd be the one wanting to marry him. We parted with a promise to see each other again soon.

David lived in one of the small houses scattered on arid, bare terrain, not far from Zikhron Ya'aqov. Seeing me, he rejoiced, though his big eyes sparkled only when he was looking at his little Shalom or his wife, Valeria. He was poor, quiet, with an inner turmoil, like our father. His beloved wife, also a survivor, had problems with her lungs, while he had some with his heart. They were not made to work on that rocky land.

Suddenly, without thinking, I told him about Gabi. . . . His reaction to my idea of getting married was overblown.

"He's a stranger, what are you saying?"

"And what about you, wanting me to marry Poppa's friend? Who knows how much longer I'll have to stay in that camp. I won't spend my life there with thirty people in one room, standing in line to eat. I still hear gunshots. For us, a sanatorium would be better than a transit camp!"

"But you don't even know who he is . . ."

"And when do you know who someone is?"

"He could be a scoundrel, a liar, a thief. Where is he from?"

"What does it matter where he's from?"

"But you're only seventeen years old . . ."

"What am I going to do with my seventeen years?"

"And him? How old is he?"

"Twenty-two. I like him. He's handsome, and from Budapest."

"And what's his trade?"

"Nothing. He's a sailor. Does anyone get to do what he wants to do?"

"You always have the right answer, don't you?"

"And what about our cousin Adele's husband who's a street cleaner? What can one do without knowing Hebrew?"

"Do what you want, you don't listen to anyone anyway! Wait. Wait until you turn eighteen and you can become a beautiful soldier and even learn the language."

"I will never hold a gun in my hand."

"You would rather be killed?"

"I think so. I prefer to have had a martyr for a father than an assassin."

"I would be a soldier for the love of Israel."

"I know. But I wouldn't. Wars bring wars. I would disarm the whole world."

"Right, you keep dreaming. At some point you'll have a rude awakening."

"I've already had that."

In the end, my beloved brother and I apologized to each other and parted reconciled, repentant, moved.

I played with the baby and we ate, drank, and after exchanging kisses and hugs I left.

A rabbi from the army married me and Gabi in the dining-room aboard Gabi's ship. We danced, sang and got "drunk" with Coke and sodas. Gabi's friend, Dov, who worked as a cook on the ship, offered us a place to live in the basement of a large villa owned by a German, who lived upstairs with his wife. There was a room available which soon became our poor love nest. The bathroom-shower-kitchen was shared with another newlywed couple who also lived there. The folding bed came from the ship, as well as a folding table and linen. Gabi's marriage-leave lasted a week, which we spent making love like two dogs unable to part. The food was provided by the cook, Dov, who was fat, small, the exact opposite of Gabi. He'd bring us whatever he could from the ship's galley. We didn't have to pay for rent or electricity. The owner of the house was a mysterious and invisible ghost. All one could sense from above was his silent hostility, against the State that had confiscated that space, and against us, its occupants. He would pace loudly overhead and listen to Mozart at a high volume, making me nostalgic for my piano lessons.

Slowly we furnished the little room with a small armoire, a table, two chairs, and even a small rug for the cement floor. I noticed that my husband had a slight nervous tic. After that week of passion, he had to leave and I knew neither where he went nor when he would return. Dov's wife, small, thin, insignificant, spoke in the Hungarian dialect of a small town, and surely wasn't Jewish. Her name was Piri, short for Piruska—the same as my schoolmate, also a survivor.

Piri suggested I go to work with her as a cleaner in the military hospital in Haifa.

"Work is work," she said.

"That's right," I answered and ended up beside the beds of wounded soldiers, eating their leftovers.

When I left, the personnel director asked me to open my bag so it could be searched, and I was mortified and offended at being treated like a thief. Again my knees trembled, my heart stuttering as if out of air.

"Don't take it personally. They check everyone, every day. That's how it is. The storage room's full of stuff and people steal shirts, sheets, pillows. It's normal."

"Not for me."

After years of sleeping on rough pallets, it seemed like paradise to have a home, though it was only a small room with a tiny window obstructed by bars, facing the courtyard at ground level; a lace curtain was enough to make the obstructed view more pleasant.

The presence of Piri, and of the other couple beyond the wall, even though they were not very communicative, helped stave off loneliness. I'd close my eyes like I did as a child, dreaming, no longer about growing up and helping my parents but about making peace with reality, about not feeling easily hurt and stripped bare by ugly looks. I'd dream about forgetting my poor mother's fable, and instead of thinking of milk and honey, I thought of the blood that was still running in this place where one learned to shoot before learning to walk! This "old" newborn country that needed care and defense, that needed youth, strength, and love to live—the same as my own needs, except I had thought I would find open arms and hearts, not armed ones. I didn't even understand why people here worked on Saturdays. On top of that, the doctors would make us clean their own apartments after they were repainted.

When Gabi came back, he immediately got upset when he learned I was working at the hospital—and that I was writing.

"What are you writing?" he shouted, grabbing the notebook from my hands.

"Something of mine."

"Let me read it."

"No, don't touch it."

"I'll shred it to pieces!" He began ripping it up.

"You can do whatever you want: rip it, burn it, but I will write it again. It's indestructible: it's written inside me and no one can ever erase it. Anyway, what's the matter with you? Why have you returned so full of anger?"

"I had a fight with my boss."

"Why?"

"Because I fell asleep."

"I went to visit Judit and David. I adore their children. Why don't we have a baby, too?"

"A baby? In such poverty? Are you crazy? You don't know what you're saying. And how would we support a child?"

"We'll make do. My mother used to say that when there is food for two, there's enough for three."

"I don't want to see you pregnant. And I don't even want to hear about having children. I want your body as it is." And he nearly threw me on the bed.

After two days he left again, without telling me where he was going. And every time he returned, he was ready to fight because of my trips to see Judit, or David, as if they would take my affection from him, though he wasn't even there. He'd also interrogate me about whom I'd met, seen, as if I'd been out having fun. He was obsessively jealous and his questioning began to annoy me. We went on like this for months.

He also disapproved of my work, so in the end I had to leave it. I went to the Café Nizza, where we'd met, to sell ice cream. In the meantime, I took a Hebrew class. And the café owner, old Ungar, suggested I also take a course in waitressing because I was a beautiful girl and would surely make good tips. Gabi hated anything I did. But his salary as a sailor wasn't sufficient. He loved his job as a mechanic and the rocking of the ship was his cradle, like my vagina was his maternal womb.

With my certificate in waitressing, I found a job in a large restaurant by the seaside promenade in Haifa. The owner was a small German Jew; his sad, thin wife was the cashier. Besides me, there were two waiters from Transylvania and three Arab Israeli who fried fish. They prepared Middle Eastern foods, washed dishes and pots, did the cleaning, and slept all together in a basement room similar to mine. I felt a natural solidarity with them, which I tried to communicate, feeling ashamed of the owner who drove them like slaves and made his wife so downcast as she sat at her cashier's post. With me, he softened his authoritarian tone. For the few words he exchanged with his wife he used German. With the numerous Arab customers from the area, he spoke Arabic. With the sailors he spoke Hebrew. With Americans, English. He had a thousand eyes and made his employees run between the tables, without stopping, overtime. The money he made in a single day, some of it in dollars, was double my yearly salary. But old Ungar was right about the tips; they were plentiful, though often accompanied by a slap on my bottom, an invitation to go for a walk, the wink of an eye. Once, an American sailor made me cry when he went too far with his hands. The restaurant owner, instead of reproaching him, got upset with me. "What are you crying for? Are you a painted egg that you can't be touched? Did he break anything? Did he hurt you?"

"Yes, yes, yes," I replied.

His wife looked at him angrily but didn't say a word. Was she afraid of that pompous windbag? I was no longer happy to go to work, though I was making good money. I wanted a more decent home, a real family, a husband who, when off duty from his military service, would be less aggressive.

One day I invited the three Arab boys to have coffee at my house and they came with a few bottles of beer, which they gave me as a gift. When I started drinking from the bottle, they screamed: "It's piss, it's piss, it's piss!" I was so stunned I could never look them in the face again.

One Friday evening Gabi threw the soup at me, complaining it was too hot. It was his first violent act. He apologized to me a thousand times, and though I ultimately forgave him, I never forgot. The second time, I could not forgive him.

It was a Saturday. Instead of waiting for him at home, I had joined Judit who was at the beach with her baby. I'd just arrived when I saw him marching toward me, furious, shouting that I was a whore who wanted to show herself in a bikini. I had my period and hadn't even undressed. He continued to insult me, calling me "whore" and kicking me repeatedly, ordering me to go back home.

"Never again," I told myself at every kick, in front of a group of families standing in the shade with their children. I loved him, but the resolution of that "never again" inside me was strong. I did not cry.

For once, not even Judit did anything in the face of that unexpected assault. It paralyzed her, and she held her baby tight, fearing Gabi could harm him as well. But he left immediately. I went home with Judit, where she reproached me for having married a crazy man.

The next day, having only the clothes I wore, I wanted to go home to fetch my things. Judit and I crept close to the little barred window, and, looking furtively inside, saw a scene of total destruction. Watching my husband fight violently but vainly to rip a pair of my nylon tights to shreds, I felt desolate.

I bought the necessary clothing and didn't miss a single day at work. Soon Gabi showed up at the restaurant with a remorseful expression, deformed by the nervous tic of his mouth. He begged me: "Mommy, my little mommy, my love, come home, I love you, I love you. I'll never touch you again, I swear, darling, believe me. Look at me. I brought you a pair of underwear, look at me."

"I can't, I can't, I only want a divorce."

"Look at what I brought you, your things."

"I just want a divorce."

"And what if I don't give it to you."

"I will report you."

"No, no, no," he murmured cravenly, "yes, yes, yes, I'll give you the divorce."

I left Judit's place and moved to a furnished room in an apartment owned by an elderly single lady, who lived near the Café Nizza. Among the tenants were three young men, a bit elusive, as if there illegally. There was also an older man, who impressed me with his intense, thoughtful look, his fine features and olive skin. They eyed me suspiciously, and once in a while they gathered together and the older man spoke furtively, conspiratorially, as if in some secret meeting of a communist cell. I heard them say: "Our father." They were talking about Stalin!

I was perplexed, disoriented, especially by that "Our father," in that tone that sounded like prayer. "Who are they?" I wondered, "What do they want?" I stopped eavesdropping on them. But at the first opportunity I asked the older man what they'd been talking about.

"Poetry," he dissembled—then gave me the most beautiful gift I've ever received: the complete poems of József Attila, my favorite, most beloved poet. And, quoting the author, he said: "My heart has already roamed round a long while, but now is taking root, understanding that only those who live can love immortally."

"What do these verses mean" I asked myself, "Why did he chose them for me?"

After shaking my hand, he turned to go—and I was sad that he'd lied to me. "It wasn't true that you were speaking about poetry!"

Briefly, the words stopped him, but before I could add anything else, with a dark expression on his face, he left. Yet, I liked him, though I wasn't sure why. I found him attractive, sensitive. But why lie to me about the meeting?

Amos, Judit's husband, who was a man of few words, explained to me that in Israel there was no communist party, but there were communist people, who weren't liked. And the party of the Orthodox Jews, which was very influential, did not tolerate atheism in the Jewish State.

"Are they persecuted?" I asked. "Isn't everyone free to be what they are if they don't harm anyone?"

"People are never what they are, and everyone adapts to the various regimes. Life is difficult outside the common herd. Socialism and democracy must be strengthened, but here what's most important is peace. To live on quicksand is nerve-wracking. Communism in reality means dictatorship. Dictators hypnotize the masses who don't think, who follow the strongest, applauding those who make promises. Dictators are plagiarists, thieves of minds, dreams, they know people's desires and tell them what they want to hear. An old game that's repeated itself since the world began."

Judit was eyeing her husband with gratitude that, for once, he didn't reject my questions or me, a woman he considered too lax and independent, someone who, in his judgment, "married and divorced as if it were a game."

My divorce was also frowned upon by my brother David, who blamed me for it. I told him I would divorce a thousand times if unhappy in marriage.

"Better to be unhappy alone than with someone else," I said.

My ex-husband asked me to remarry him several times, bringing me gifts like a straw bag from Naples, a shell necklace from Genoa. Although I was not indifferent to him, as soon as I'd notice that tic at the corner of his mouth I'd say, "No, no, and no." And he'd immediately go on the offensive then, making fun of my job as a waitress, waving a picture of me he kept in his wallet as a demonstration of his love.

One day, as I was returning home from work, the old landlady, a woman who spoke Yiddish in a lilting Polish tone, approached me looking agitated: the police had come and taken the three boys; she did not know where, or if they would return. I grew specially concerned for the older tenant who gave me the book of poems, whom I'd have liked to get to know better, to talk to him, read the poems with him as I used to do with Endre in my previous life. I anxiously awaited his return but didn't dare go to the police. I detested uniforms—even the sight of Amos in his traffic-police uniform bothered me. By chance, Amos was covering the area around the Café Nizza where I spent most of my time. He informed me that, since my official residence was with them, a notice for me had arrived at their house about my military service, which would have to be done now that I was divorced. Judit and David also said it was inevitable.

"What if I marry again?" I replied.

"Are you out of your mind? With whom?"

"Anyone. A family check would always be convenient to have. I can't be a soldier."

"Maybe you'll learn the language well, and a trade," they repeated.

"I can't stand living in a dorm and taking orders. No, no, and no."

At the Café Nizza, there was another sailor I'd known for some time. His name was Tomi Bruck and he immediately accepted my proposal. I had made arrangements with an agent for a dance company, and soon after celebrating our fake wedding I divorced and left for Athens with the company. The pay was good, the agent was a Jewish man, his wife a soloist dancer, and together they'd created the troupe. I wasn't quite sure what I could do, but it all seemed fabulous to me. To see Athens, travel, dance—it was all a dream. The troupe consisted of a blond gypsy, a sulking German girl, an older woman, and the agent's wife, who was the only professional dancer.

We started with rehearsals, which lasted all day. Soon I found myself on an airplane, my first flight—it seemed *I* was flying. My family was scandalized. The novelty of my new circumstances did unsettle me, but without undermining my true self, in which my past continued to ferment, always present. Was I running away from my marriage, military service, or from my disappointment with a deaf world?

As a child I'd wanted to become a ballerina or acrobat. I studied dance in school and was good at it. I had so many projects my mother disapproved of. There were so many things I wanted to do, but until then I had only done what I could—not the one thing I wanted: to write . . . a book, a diary, yet I hadn't taken pencil in hand again . . . how long had it been? Maybe I did everything wrong, or simply found myself in the wrong world? For Judit and David I was a lost person, a dancer!

Escape

I MAY HAVE BEEN the saddest dancer Athens ever saw, backed by three gray Jewish musicians who played waltzes by Strauss, making their violins cry. Four of us danced with the air of survivors, twirling round in long, loose, white gowns. We vaguely resembled lost birds with our wide sleeves raised, fluttering here and there, bumping into each other. People applauded as we hovered like white clouds in those gloomy clubs where I even saw King Faruk. The problem was having to drink with clients when invited. I hated alcohol, didn't drink wine or any aperitif. But I didn't have money to break my contract and leave the group, so I learned to furtively spill my champagne on the floor in the dark.

In the barely decent hotel, I shared a room with the blue-eyed Gypsy woman. She was joyful, protective, and the daughter of a musician from Budapest. And, like me, she had divorced a Jewish man. We became inseparable. She wasn't very beautiful, and

I—younger, prettier, the most invited in our slightly improved dance troupe—would drag her with me.

Athens and the sea were enchanting, like the popular Greek songs and dances—the sly, lying eyes of Greek men not so much.

The finest thing that happened to me there, that restored my sense of self, was being invited for a Jewish holiday by some well-off families who treated us with kind curiosity.

After Athens, we went to Istanbul, a large, hectic, and beautiful city with lively markets and a spectacular sea. Fortunately, Muslim men didn't drink alcohol, but they treated us ambiguously and at times made approaches aggressively, even violently.

I became friends with the owner of the club, a kind, respectful man whose ill father looked like a sacred icon. I kept him company whenever I could. I liked to hold his thin, trembling hand, and would clean his sweaty forehead while he seemed enlivened at each gesture I made.

At the club I had a solo piece—not so much dancing as singing, in English, after which I'd run to the old man who smiled at me with tender gratitude.

"He has cancer," his son told me. "He once was a great pianist."

It seemed like they lived alone in their house. Are they really father and son? I wondered, noticing something strange and feminine about the young man: he wore nail polish.

One day, during the brief time I spent at the hotel, I realized a man was observing me. He was rather short and seemed timid, serious. Suddenly a woman appeared next to him, plain-looking but full of energy, and also began staring at me. Soon I realized they were speaking in Hungarian. It seemed she was encouraging him to approach me, insisting, even pushing him in my direction before turning to leave the hotel.

"I'm Max," said the man, "I have a dance company called Max Group. I'd like you to dance with us. We're about to leave for Zurich. Our girls are all professionals. My wife is a ballerina and choreographer. We have several Austrian dancers, one from Hungary, and a Chinese contortionist. Our girls aren't allowed to drink. I myself take them back to the hotel after the show. They're all well-paid and always dance in first-class clubs. Can I call you by your first name? Would you like to join us? One of our girls even has her brother with her. Our company is respectable and well-known."

He sounded convincing and I immediately accepted his offer. I was able to get out of my engagement with the other troupe. I was only sorry to be separated from my Gypsy friend, Jolanka, but Max didn't want her. Our long hug in parting was not goodbye, we continued to keep in touch from a distance.

I was also sad to leave the old man and his son, Gùndüz, but Zurich was more familiar to me, more western—and later we'd be heading to Naples. I thought Italy was the center of the world. All Max's promises were true. If anything, the strictness with the girls seemed exaggerated, too harsh: it was rigorously forbidden to sit and drink with clients after the show.

In the hotel I roomed with the Chinese girl, who had a grace and beauty truly rare. There was also the slender, ethereal Elfi, with her brother. And Lili, the heavier one who was a belly dancer. Max's wife, Helen, was the teacher with stick in hand. I was having a lot of trouble with a piece we all did together, a mambo. The skilled musicians accompanied me while I sang *Because of you* and *Rainbow*. It was all much better than being a cleaner in the hospital or carrying dishes piled on one arm while having to deal with a tyrannical boss. Zurich seemed very clean, cold, and white after chaotic, beautiful, and colorful Istanbul. The people were reserved, buttoned-up, their applause rather lukewarm. Their German, though different in pronunciation and tone from the German I knew, was still slightly disturbing. In our troupe the common language was English, which everyone spoke badly, but we could communicate. My roommate communicated mostly by smiling and seemed totally infatuated with herself, her image, eying her reflection in the large mirror of our room where she practiced contortions, moving like a snake. Even in our company there weren't real friendships. I got a bit closer with Lili, the Jewish woman who'd left a small child with her Austrian husband in Vienna.

"But how were you able to marry an Austrian?"

I dared ask her. She didn't answer, but only blushed with a somewhat defeated, resigned expression.

The city seemed as neutral now as it had been in the war. It looked bare, without kiosks, smells of spices, or voices ringing out with music from cafés. Odorless, colorless. Men passing in suits and ties didn't turn with voluptuous eyes to watch women as in Athens or Istanbul. And women, well-dressed but in vaguely masculine style, seemed stolid and firm, without the softness of Turkish or Greek women. After the ambiguous, inscrutable faces of the noisy cities we'd lived in previously, with all their splendid monuments and rituals, introverted Zurich intimidated us, made us walk almost on tiptoes, smiling timidly during our performances as we adapted to a city that felt foreign, perhaps not quite welcoming. On the streets there were no beggars, rowdy boys, or men whistling at us. This cold climate, as if contagious, also conditioned our relationships, which were non-existent. No confidences, no friendships; only rehearsals, discipline, boredom and loneliness. Would military service have been better?

One Two Three,
One Two Three. . . .

FROM ORDERLY ZURICH we arrived in sunny Naples, relieved.

The city itself, the people, air, and sky were all smiling. We were immediately warned to be aware of our bags and not to trust people we didn't know. This prejudice about a place so pleasant and vibrant disturbed me. The Santa Lucia *pensione* near the boardwalk looked like paradise, and the club, Casina Delle Rose, only a few steps away, the garden of Eden. From my small single room I could see the sign of a restaurant, Zi' Teresa. Inside, beyond the glass, people were hypnotized by the television screen, the totem, miraculous object, recently arrived in Italy, now emitting sounds of a guitar and a voice singing about a certain "Maruzzella."

For the first time I felt immediately at home, after such a long, sad pilgrimage. "Here I am," I told myself: "this is my country." The word "homeland" has never passed my lips: in the name of "homeland" people have committed all sorts of crimes. I would abolish the word—as well as other words like "mine," "be quiet," "obey," "the law is equal for everyone," "nationalism," "racism," "war," perhaps even "love" when emptied of its substance.

New words were needed to speak about Auschwitz as well, a new language, one that would hurt less than my mother tongue. The language of that song about Maruzzella was totally unknown to me. The first word I learned in Italian was "ciao," which I heard from the girl who was cleaning my room. "Ciao," I replied, and she laughed at the way I pronounced the "o."

The club, which perhaps even Max wasn't familiar with, was outdoors in a large garden lush with flowers under a sky full of stars. Beneath an eave there was a bar, and in the middle, a dance floor with tables all around. It was May, my birth-month. Everything seemed enchanting. I was almost coming to peace with life—not my past life but the one surrounding me now with that sun, that sea, which, perhaps, would never make me throw up again. At sunset, the blue-eyed owner, who was hiring a dance troupe for the first time, became emotional when he saw us, as we did with him. The news about the dance was reported in a local newspaper, and posters with our picture were all over town. Seeing them I felt ashamed, as if I were back home and someone might recognize me. Finally, on the first Saturday after our arrival, after many rehearsals, now with a lighting director, we debuted in the garden filled with families, men, women, children, young and old. Our piece was accompanied by South American music, then Arabic music for the belly dancer and classical for young Elfi, who looked like an angel. People clapped enthusiastically and repeatedly, we bowed several times.

In that city of song I was no longer singing, as we no longer had an orchestra. The music, mostly danceable, came from records with American songs, Frank Sinatra, and famous Italian singers of the time.

People at the tables drank beer, wine, and sometimes whiskey. We were free to stay or leave. The club's owner asked our "custodian" Max if we could stay a little longer because some young men wished to dance with us, including two famous actors who wanted a dance with me: Ugo Tognazzi and Walter Chiari. He kept saying their names, which didn't mean anything to me. The one named Tognazzi held me tight, slyly, while saying words in Italian like *radio*, *Io*, *programma*, constantly displaying his shorts fingers and repeating *uno, due, tre*. And so I learned to count to three in Italian, my first lesson. In time I would write all my verses and books in this language, starting with my first book published more than sixty years ago.

To me Naples seemed poor, rich, degraded, a deeply human yet unreal city, full of voices. At the markets they tried to sell all kinds of merchandise, flourishing figurines from the nativity scene under your nose: shepherds, Baby Jesus, the Virgin Mary, angels, the popular actors Totò and the De Filippo Trio, good-luck horns. It wasn't easy to be rid of the seller. In that noble, loud city, it wasn't rare for a man to kiss your hand and for singing to pour from homes, like a fantasy. Vendors yelling, baskets lowered from windows, clothes hanging across alleyways everywhere.

To be tourists, foreigners, in a city or country isn't the same thing as living there, one stays on the surface, perhaps—but even that is something. I couldn't find a trace of the Italian "Latin lover." I only met three men who wanted "to show me something," I had no idea what, but—apart from the kissing of my hand, which I found embarrassing—they didn't even come close to touching me. A redheaded man, who was strongly nearsighted, brought me to Herculaneum, where I stood stunned as he, gesturing wildly, explained what happened in 79 AD: "Pompeii, Herculaneum, kaput!" he said with a slight stutter. I had never seen such destruction—worse than bombed Berlin and Dresden! Finally, in a used-clothes market, the poor man insisted on buying me a white skirt which cost five hundred lire and, in order not to offend him, I accepted, thanking him as if it were something precious.

Another suitor brought me to the enchanting Amalfi coast. A third, an aristocratic brunet dressed all in white, to the island of Ischia: "Sant'Angelo" he kept saying beside the sea, at the foot of the mountain.

After Zurich, I thought I was in Wonderland— although the first time we went to the beach in Naples in bikinis we were expelled by policemen who eyed us maliciously, pointing at our skimpy bikinis as young men laughed and argued with them, seeming to say, "Leave them alone!" while ogling our bodies.

Later, we were told that in Italy women weren't yet wearing bikinis, that they still wore one-piece bathing suits. And I wondered if they were less evolved than in Greece? I would understand it in Turkey, where women were all covered up, but Italy? With all the naked figures in paintings and women's cleavage showing everywhere, weren't they more provocative than us? It seemed rather strange to me. . . .

To learn about fascist Italy, ally to Hitler's Germany, there were the films of the great Neorealists: Rossellini, De Sica, De Santis . . . showing the history, customs, and culture with sound-images that could have been just as powerful silent, like the films of Chaplin.

For someone who couldn't read books in Italian, cinema and television were the best schools to learn the language, along with songs, and the extroverted Neapolitans who mimed their words. After a couple of months, having a certain ease with languages and armed with courage to speak, though still badly, I was already speaking Italian and people corrected me when I made mistakes.

In Naples, as if magically, Lili, the belly dancer, began a relationship with an aristocratic Sicilian lawyer, with Max's approval. The Chinese woman stayed with Max, the evanescent Elfi went back to Vienna with her brother. The lawyer wanted me to stay with Lili in Rome until their wedding and found us an apartment in Via Vaina 8. He promised her he'd arrange to have her son move to Italy as well.

Rome! Center of the world! No more dance. Freedom! After vibrant Naples, the Eternal City, true to its name, seemed to have existed since time immemorial, like Jerusalem. The lawyer, Simon, stayed with us for a few days, showing us around like a tour guide. He didn't really need to talk as our eyes were mesmerized, by the frescos of the Sistine Chapel, the piazzas, palaces, the churches we briefly visited, the Tiber splitting the city in two. And Saint Peter's, with Pope Pius XII who struck a hieratic pose, as if absorbed by faith, or, perhaps, sick.

In the alleys and neighborhoods, on the walls, there were still signs of the war, despite the several years that had already gone by.

The city was majestic, but there were more beggars than in Naples. Simon explained that Italy was one-and-three, like the Trinity: the South, which he preferred for its human warmth; the center, with the Vatican, attracting people from all over, including migrants from the rest of Italy; and the North, richer and colder, also from a human point of view. But all of Italy was beautiful—and the lawyer clarified that Jews had been in Rome before there even were Romans. He showed us the ghetto, the large synagogue where I'd already been on my own. Looking at it, I felt like crying, it made me feel lost there in the heart of Catholicism. I felt a painful nostalgia for my family, as I had during Passover in Greece. I also missed Judit and David, and promised myself to visit them soon.

Simon and Lili were gathering the documents for their civil marriage. He was going back and forth to Sicily, she was calm and serene. They already seemed like a close-knit older couple, whispering rather than talking to each other. She gazed at him with loyal eyes, like a loving dog; he, short and plump, with a small head, was more reassuring than good-looking. Together they emanated an air of peace and tranquility, a natural connection as if they'd known each other not merely a few months, but all their lives. She aroused intimate, conspicuously sensual thoughts, of her amber skin shining with oil or the sweat of love. He was always in light-colored clothing, neatly shaven and perfumed, with straight, well-combed hair. He looked like a privileged and pampered child.

In his Roman apartment she was always in bed eating, with an apathetic air. Being with her was like being alone, she was inscrutable, hardly uttering a word, and would only go out when Simon came back. Otherwise, she lay in bed as if anesthetized, indifferent to everything. I couldn't understand how she'd ever ended up on the dance floor where she'd moved languidly, like a hypnotized sleepwalker.

"What's your child's name?" I asked her.

"Simon," she softly replied.

Was it the name that sealed her attachment to that middle-aged man? Was he still a bachelor or was he divorced? Did he have children? I knew nothing about him; perhaps she alone knew something. Together they were two whispering tombs and I felt suffocated if I didn't speak with someone, do something. I felt totally useless. I enrolled in an English class, and an old spinster, like the one who taught me piano at my sister Sara's house, gave me lessons in Italian grammar; I would go crazy memorizing all those past-tense verbs: *ebbi, ebbero, fossero, fossi, fu. . . .*

My English was fairly good, though it was against my wishes that they put me in the most advanced course, where my first homework was on Shakespeare's Macbeth.

Finally, I took up the little notebook that I had abandoned and began to write in Italian, this: "I was born in a small Hungarian village . . ."

The wait for the documents seemed endless, and Lili left for Sicily with Simon. I ended up in a furnished room near the Spanish steps, paying sixteen-thousand lire a month with an extra two-hundred to use the shower. The room was dark and faced an internal courtyard infested with mice rummaging through the garbage. In the vestibule were pictures of Pius XII, King Umberto and Mussolini. The landlady, Signora Ida, scrutinized me as if I were an alien. With a voice hoarse from bronchitis, she followed me everywhere and had a morbid curiosity. At night she gossiped with her daughter and meek husband. Then they'd go to a nearby café to watch the television that loomed from above—people bought television-sets in installments, like washing-machines or vacuum-cleaners. In the evening, alone and in silence, I'd write under the weak ceiling-light until being interrupted by Signora Ida who, back from the café, would scold me, saying that I should eat, have dinner with them or go out to eat at Otello's in Via della Croce, where people from the world of cinema hung out.

"You are a beautiful young woman, go out, show yourself around, and maybe you'll be an actress. What are you doing there writing all the time? You'll become blind."

After a while I took her advice and would eat with them, a soup made with beans or cabbage, or would go to Otello's where tables lining both sides of the room were connected and one never ate alone.

Once I happened to sit next to a certain Tonino—his last name was Cervi, I later learned—who was with an elegant lady, well-groomed and smelling of hairspray. She said her name was Nadia and shook my hand. I noticed how finely manicured her nails were, and soon discovered she was a famous seamstress. She asked me what languages I spoke, besides my Italian which was greatly improving.

"English, German, and a bit of French."

"Perfect." Turning to Tonino, she told him I could replace Sylvie—then promised me a job, if I were available.

"Yes, yes," I replied.

In a few days I found myself working as manager of a beauty salon in Via Condotti, replacing Sylvie, a French woman who'd returned to Paris. The owner, Signora G., who always spoke and behaved brusquely, unpleasantly, said she'd opened this famous salon in partnership with a young hairdresser with golden hands, discovered by her. Every day she listed my tasks: cashier duties and taking care of the telephone, appointments, the clients' robes, the magazines, orders at the bar, sales at the boutique, replenishing products, supervising employees, presenting her the daily receipts, entertaining the clients according to their importance—before they were seen by the hairdresser with the golden hands—making sure to treat with velvet-gloves actors and actresses, princesses, top models, rich escorts, soubrettes, and especially Princess Torlonia and Paola Ruffo di Calabria, Valentina Cortese and Anna Magnani, who had the most intense face I've ever seen. "Make the nouveau riche and the vulgar ones wait. Did you understand everything? Everything? Why don't you answer? Are you scared? If you do your job well you stay, otherwise you go. Here you're among the crème de la crème of Rome, and you need to know how to comport yourself. If Mastroianni or another cinema star comes to dye their hair for a film, you'll stay overtime at their discretion. Is that clear? Did you understand everything?" she kept repeating.

"Yes, ma'am."

"*Yes, ma'am* my foot. Stop talking with that gape of an orphan."

I was stunned. I preferred a million times over to have a male boss. Women were worse than men even in the camps—but eighty-thousand lire a month was a lot for me. The work was a lot, too, at least twelve hours a day, sometimes more if celebrities came. I met Delia Scala, Franca Valeri, Lea Massari, Sandra Milo, Flora Mastroianni, Zsa Zsa Gabor, Princess Margaret, Elsa Martinelli, and many other ladies, intimate friends of Signora G., who fancied herself a socialist.

Only on Sunday could I return to writing. During the week I ran back and forth in the various departments of the salon. In the evening, with swollen feet, aching all over I'd collapse in bed after a cup of tea and piece of bread, like when I was a child. Sometimes I ate at Otello's, spending a thousand lire; I'd become friendly with Otello's wife and daughters, and everyone there treated me like family. At work, I also became friends with a Dutch woman who came to sell her long hair—we made wigs there as well, for men and women.

At that time, Italy was entering the so-called economic boom and the proceeds at the end of the day would amount to around two-million lire. But I was beginning to have trouble; I couldn't keep up with it all. When Signora G. would arrive later in the morning, she'd greet me with: "Piece of shit, go and put on some makeup!"

Everyone feared her foul language and unbearable character, but she also had moments of generosity. And, people murmured, she even suffered the pain of love.

I was also hurt by the arrogance of Martinelli, who, stomping her feet, reminded me to call her Countess Martinelli Scotti.

Nobody knew anything about me, my experiences, my past. Once in a while, Signora G. scolded me if I didn't smile at clients or looked sad—a sadness I had to repress, just as I had to endure her humiliations. Often, she'd ask, "What's that funeral face? Here you have to smile even if you don't feel like it. And leave your fucking business outside. These bitches, only a few of them real ladies, should be pampered. Clear?!"

At Otello's, I'd become acquainted with an Armenian refugee who was a literary critic, and one day I found him in the company of another man. He introduced me to the man, a poet and director who asked me immediately about my book. But I was mesmerized by his face, his erudite eyes and full lips; enchanted by his voice that used the aristocratic "r," which I could have listened to forever; by his agitated hands with soft, delicate palms I wished to feel forever; and the beautifully shaped fragile face I couldn't bear to lose sight of. In that moment he entered my soul, emptied me of all energy, made my knees tremble. Such immediate, irrational, mysterious yet absolute feeling scared me. All this for someone whose name wasn't even known to me (I honestly hadn't caught it), whose very being confused me. I felt I'd been plunged into something unfathomable from which I'd never emerge.

Nelo, this chosen man among millions, would give himself to me and disappear. Would look for me to then abandon me. Would want me, and then wouldn't.

Between the desired "yes" and unexpected "no," time seemed to elude us, as in a prison from which neither of us would escape for the next sixty years of joy, passion, suffering, tenderness, patience, pain, loving each other in good health and sickness, until his last breath in my arms.

Soon after we began living together he asked me to leave the salon, where, from reading magazine articles, they'd learned about my just published first book. Martinelli ran to Signora G. to show her my picture on the cover of a popular magazine, and the soubrette Delia Scala showed an article with pictures of my family, found after the war in manure piled at the edge of our courtyard.

"Why didn't you say anything about yourself? You're a real bitch!" Signora G. kept screaming, "You never said you were a writer! You never said who you are! A real bitch!"

"I'm leaving, just give me my severance pay."

"What? You don't even have a work permit. I'll have you deported."

"I have the right to be compensated," I replied with a stern and judgmental glare.

She seemed to understand the look and, lowering her eyes, said, "Alright, alright, go to Giorgio the bookkeeper! He'll give you something." In fact, he gave me a third of what they owed me.

As soon as I got home Nelo scolded me: "Never accept exploitation and humiliations. Can you explain to me why you didn't leave earlier?"

"Yes, because I needed to work."

"First dignity and freedom."

"Fine words . . ."

The day of our wedding came, at City Hall on the Capitoline Hill, officiated by Francesco Fausto Nitti, one of the founders of the anti-fascist Resistance movement *Giustizia e Libertà*.

After the brief ceremony we all went back to our work: Nelo to his poems or the editing of a film or documentary; I to the many engagements I've continued to have since that time. Journalism, TV, novels, poems, cinema, speaking about the Shoah. Trips to see family members who are no longer alive but lived in all corners of the world with their eternal nostalgia for Israel, in a new Diaspora: Miriam in Brooklyn; Judit, who after moving between Argentina and America wanted to be buried in the Holy Land, where she flew when she was about to die; Sara, who asked my forgiveness twenty years after she slapped me and now rests in Argentine soil; and David in the rust-red ground of Brazil. Their children are also all scattered.

Judit's beautiful daughter, Deborah, born nine years after Haim, was—according to my sister, my twin in the afterlife—given to her by God himself, so my mother's name would survive. As fortune had it, she'd end up living in Italy, not far from me.

"You have your books, but don't have children," Judit would say every time she came to Rome, as if in comparison to her children my books were nothing.

"Books are children as well," I'd reply, knowing she'd look at me with eyes that suggested "poor thing."

As an adopted daughter of Italy, which has given me more than my daily bread, I am and will always be grateful. Yet, today I'm very worried for this country, and for Europe. I feel doubly the toxic wind blowing in the air, polluted by new forms of fascism, racism, nationalism, antisemitism. These are poisonous plants which have never been eradicated and are sprouting again with new branches, their bitter leaves feeding the people who listen to those screaming in their name, who are hungry for a strong identity, for a loud, pure, white Italian-ness. How sad, how dangerous it is.

My own identity has been somehow destabilized lately. Instead of being happy for the *laurea honoris causa*, the awards, the nomination to the Hungarian Academy, I have felt something unexpected. Resentment? Perhaps—towards a world which, once an assassin, chose to exclude me from society, wanting to suppress me.

And I ask myself: "Is all this for the writer, or is this compensation to the survivor, from those who owe me nothing?"

I hardly recognized myself, always invited to ceremonies where I question who I am in the midst of crowds, applause, orators, ministers, provosts, professors, regional governors, mayors, bishops, red cross nurses, firefighters, police, volunteers, musicians, citizens and selfie, selfie, selfie. . . .

"Who are they talking about?!" I wondered.

Embarrassed, confused, separated from myself, doubled, and perhaps also gratified, while walking on the red carpet I felt a painful nostalgia for the little girl, running barefoot in the tepid dusty air of spring on the little street of Six Houses, where I was simply ME, with no past, only future, a lifetime ago. Not the protagonist of a sort of fable, next to a provost draped in an ermine cloak, and I in a black gown with white collar like a privileged child.

If I think about it, it seems the most wonderful game I ever played.

Letter to God

SINCE THE FIRST LETTER I wrote You in my mind when I was nine, more than eighty years have passed! And I blushed both then and two nights ago for an idea that has never abandoned me.

It seemed to me a blasphemy I never dared express, perhaps shamelessness or lucid folly, but now I am truly writing to You, as long as I am able to see.

I write to You, who will never read my scribbles, will never answer my questions, my thoughts of a lifetime.

Elementary thoughts, small ones, belonging to the child who is still in me. They did not grow up or old with me, they did not even change much. Perhaps I feel the urgency to put in writing what I have accumulated in my mind because life is depriving me of my sight. I already have enough trouble trying to decipher my crooked handwriting and drunken lines, but I am in a rush, time is running out. I am realizing that every word and line tends to rise higher and higher and, who knows, maybe they will at last reach

125

all the way to You, assuming You exist, or maybe You are made of silence, invisible and without image to the people to whom I belong. Daughter of a mother who spoke more words to You than to her six children or her husband, guilty because poor.

Children given to her by You, according to my mother, who reached out to You for everything she needed: shoes, coats, flour, meat for the Holy Saturday, sugar to replace saccharine for our tea at dinner. There was nothing she would not ask You: wood for the cold stove, a new roof for the house, an early spring, milder winter, boots for Poppa, a road less muddy to save his soles during his business trips— and that he would not come back as he usually did, empty-handed.

I confess that I was irritated by her requests, her constant talking to You annoyed me. You, who never helped even to ease her constipation, when all red-faced from the strain she held my hands, invoking You.

I thought that in that rotten wood shack she should not even mention Your name. But she would say that You were everywhere. Yet if You were everywhere, being the Only One, if everywhere then You were nowhere, because one is one. I already knew how to count before going to school, and how to read and write. I have always written, and when, as a child, I could not because I only had the school notebook, I would write in my thoughts to everyone, including You. To my father, who never played with me and only kissed me for the first time in his uniform when he went to war. He looked sad but also stood straighter than usual, more handsome, taller, while my mother, instead, was crumbling in on herself.

Maybe a year had passed since that first fatherly kiss when he gave me the second one, returning from the war with a dark expression, crushed, sweaty and aged. He felt humiliated at having been expelled from the army only because he was a Jew. In my silent thoughts in bed, I also wrote to my mother, telling her that Poppa often says the right things—although she did not think so, as if a poor father could not be right. She negated not only him but even his paternity: insisting that You had given her us children. And she delivered them when You wanted.

In my imaginary letters I asked Momma why, if Poppa had nothing to do with our being born, was he responsible for supporting us?

Of You, instead, I thought every night of my life. I questioned You on many things but never heard Your voice like Moses. You never deigned me a single answer, never deigned to answer my mother, who had absolute faith in You. The opposite of me, full of doubts, at the mercy of our small village since I opened my eyes to the world, a world that with the utmost naturalness made us the enemy. And if You saw everything, were everything, eyes, ears, how could you not notice our travails? Do you know what my father did to survive? With a rented cart he transported livestock to the city for other people: poultry, calves, and even pigs which made my mother shiver. He would leave at night to be there at dawn and would come back more depressed than triumphant because he would cede to the first buyer, being totally unfit for business. People thought he would be good at it by virtue of being Jewish, but he was impatient and was happy to make a small profit. Moreover, he had a good nature and was a dreamer, promising himself and us that one day he would have his own cart, with at least one horse.

I have always wondered, and have yet to find an answer: what's the purpose of prayers if they don't change anything or anyone, if You cannot do anything and cannot hear, or see? Or are You the invention of a superior, unfathomable mind? Or did you invent Yourself? I, who have always written without stopping, day after day, now suddenly do stop with my hand suspended in air, eyes staring in empty space. It is in this emptiness that I search for You.

We have neither Purgatory nor Paradise, but I have known Hell, where Mengele's finger would point to the left, which was fire, or right, which was agony at work-camps, experiments and death from hunger and cold.

Survival did not happen due to one's merit, but often at the cost of others' lives or in the service of the enemy. Why didn't You break that finger? In the Sistine Chapel You point towards Adam—man in Hebrew—like that doctor who ordered the Yes and the No, taking Your place. Why did You let him replace You? Let him point with his burning finger at millions of innocents who invoked You and adored You like my mother. Didn't You fear they would reject You? Or did you point Your finger against Your very

Self, following the destiny of Your elected people? As we left that Hell we were abandoned to ourselves, but You are not mortal, are You, our Eternal One? Beautiful words, full of consoling hopes, necessary as bread for those who are hungry—and the world is full of hunger, as well as plenty for only a few.

Justice is a word that should disappear from dictionaries and should not be pronounced in vain, like Your name. But You have many names and even from my mouth, sometimes, there escapes an "Oh my God!" but only in a whisper, when Evil is unbearable and I am outraged by what has happened, is happening, will happen.

Everything repeats itself. You too are the One Infinite Repetition, the greatest mystery there is, if You exist: this is the question which will never be answered. Either one believes in You blindly or doubts You rationally—or the question remains suspended between me and me.

Oh, You, the Great Silence, if only You knew my fears, of everything but not of You. If I survived, there must be some sense in it, mustn't there?

I beg You, for the first time I am asking You for something: for memory, which is my daily bread, for me, Your unfaithful believer, don't leave me in darkness. I still have young minds to illuminate in schools and university classrooms, where as a survivor I have been talking for a lifetime about my experiences. Where the most frequent questions are three: if I believe in You; if I forgive the Evil; and if I hate my torturers. To the first question I blush, as if they had asked me to stand naked; to the second I explain that a Jew can forgive only for herself, but I am not able to forgive because I think about all those who were annihilated and who wouldn't forgive me. Only to the last I have a clear answer: compassion, yes, towards anyone. Hatred, never. And therefore I am saved, orphan and free, and for this I thank You, Hashem in the Bible, Adonai in prayer, God every day.

Edith
Bruck

Author's Note

AT THE FIRST SIGN of forgetfulness, which for anyone else might be a normal event, given my age, I panicked, breathless, needing oxygen as if I were losing life itself.

"How do you write? How do you do it?" I asked in alarm to Olga, the Ukrainian woman who after my beloved husband's departure stayed by my side. I can't live alone, and she is like a good sister to me.

"I write with a pen," she answered, without quite understanding my sense of loss.

"I write by hand, then type with my old Olivetti. But you, on what do you write?" I was looking for a word I couldn't find in my otherwise lucid mind, with its legendary memory.

"Computer"—she mentioned the word that had escaped me, perhaps because I don't use it?

Anyway, in that moment, I got scared and decided to fly in reverse over my existence, just in time, being at the edge of the end that looms just beyond the door. I, who used to have the eye of a hawk, now victim of maculopathy. And today, even to me it seems unreal that I walked such a long path, which seems a fable in the dark woods of the twentieth century, with its long shadow into the third millennium.

I would like to thank Olga Ushchak, my guardian angel, and Eugenio Murrali, a young writer, who gave me his hands, eyes, and patient assistance in transferring my manuscript to a computer file.

A special thank you to my precious and attentive reader Michela Meschini. Good fate brought us together, never to be parted, at the University of Macerata where she works.

The verses quoted in the epigraph are from Nelo Risi's poem "La neve nell'armadio" in *Tutte le poesie*. Milan: Mondadori, 2020.

Interview with Edith Bruck

by Gabriella Romani

GABRIELLA ROMANI Let's start with the title, *Lost Bread*, an expression that evokes many meanings: the bread that your mother was unable to cook the morning your family was deported, a daily ritual on the table of many people but also, more symbolically, a daily presence in your creative life as a writer. Can you explain what the idea of bread means to you and how it inspired you in writing your latest book?

EDITH BRUCK I think that bread was the most important thing in my youth and still is today. All my life it has been the most important food. My mother used to say that when there is bread there is everything. And at some level I identify my mother with bread. Also, because she used to make bread, she kneaded it, she smelled of flour, her apron smelled of flour and therefore, for me, she was symbolically my bread. And for her, the most important thing was to provide bread for her children but that became really difficult, especially in the last two years of our life in the village, because there was a terrible anti-Semitism. In fact, that last precious flour was a gift from a neighbor. We had nothing, not even flour. Not having flour meant that there was nothing to eat. It was very difficult. Still today, for me bread is a precious item. The problem is that young people today do not understand the value of bread, they do not fully understand the full value of life, they play with death, they play with bread on the table. They do not appreciate what they have in life. Looking back, I think that the "no" I received in my childhood made me stronger, for later as well, in the camps. Perhaps the hard and strict life I had as a child was very helpful for me during my deportation.

GR In your book, you mention an encounter in Greece with members of the local Jewish community who invite you to their seder for Passover. I wonder what your relationship was with the local Roman Jewish community when you settled in Rome in the mid-1950s. You were coming from an Ashkenazi tradition, while the local one was mainly Roman and Sephardic. As an Ashkenazi Jew settled in Rome, did you feel you fit in?

EB The Jewish community in Rome is very closed. Very Roman, more Roman than the Romans. They have been here for a long time. I spoke about it with a friend, also a writer, Lia Levi, who is from Turin and she has also never been fully accepted in Rome. But for thirty years she was the director of the Jewish periodical *Shalom*, and therefore, in some ways she was working from within the Roman Jewish community. For me, instead, it has been more difficult, until a couple of years ago. It was even difficult to present my books in the community. Because it is a completely different world, that does not recognize you, does not know what the Yiddish culture is, does not understand the Yiddish language. It is mainly a Sephardic community. I was shocked when they asked me to bring two witnesses who could confirm my Jewishness, when I decided to be registered in the community. I was deeply offended. What did they mean by asking me if I were Jewish? I was stunned. And I have worked in journalism for many years and there are several things they never forgave me for, because the Roman community overall is very pro-Israel. All that Israel does is good for them, not for me, not everything, and I want to have the freedom to say what I really think about Israel or Palestine. But there is a price for this, not only in Rome or Israel, everywhere. And I paid for it. But lately things have changed, especially after the recent visits of Pope Francis and the Chief Rabbi in Rome, Riccardo Di Segni, and, two or three years ago, of the President of the Union of Italian Jewish Communities, Noemi Di Segni, to whom I dedicated my latest poetry book. She brought me gifts for Passover, it had never happened before, I was very moved. I had never met her before. It was a sort of reconciliation, but even after that I can't say that the Roman Jewish community and I are on very friendly terms.

GR When did you decide to register your name with the Roman Jewish community?

EB I decided to sign my name up in 1972, after the Israeli athletes were killed in Munich. I felt a strong desire to be part of the Jewish community. Naturally, I was never "out" of the Jewish community and will never leave it. I feel a strong sense of belonging, though perhaps differently from other people. The interesting thing is that when the Chief Rabbi came to visit me, he asked me if I was registered in the community. I was perplexed by that question. There must be no more than 1600 people registered and he did not know if I was one of them? Perhaps my books were never popular among Jewish readers here. I am who I am and will never change. For sure, it saddens me to hear that a Jew died in a war in Israel, and it saddens me as well if a Palestinian dies, but I clearly feel closer to the people I belong to. But I am never indifferent when someone dies, whoever that person is.

GR You have lived in Italy and written in Italian since the late 1950s. What's your relationship with the Italian language and literature? Do you think that Italian defines you as a writer, or do your writings somehow transcend any identity or national definition?

EB I can say immediately that the Italian language for me represents salvation. It's my refuge, my complete freedom to say what I want. It has no deep roots for me, as Hungarian has instead. If I say bread in Hungarian, *kenyér*, I think of my mother, and tragic memories come to my mind. I see her with her apron and all the rest. If I say bread in Italian, *pane*, I think of the bakery where I buy it, of its fragrance but nothing else. It does not mean much to me, it does not make me cry. While bread in Hungarian still hurts. Not only the word "bread," but also the insults, the swear words in Hungarian, they hurt. Perhaps I would not have written all these books if I did not have another language to use. I don't know. Language for me is everything I am, my identity, my home. Perhaps if people listened to us, welcomed us after the war, I would not have written all these books. Who knows? But I know for sure that I have been wanting to write since I was a child. I wanted to be a poet. I told my mother and she replied: Sure, if you want to starve. She was probably right. In 1946 I began to write in Hungarian. Some people suggested that Primo Levi pushed me to write. Absolutely not true! I did not even know him when I began to write. But I had to destroy my first manuscript when I left Hungary illegally. Then, once I arrived in Italy, after learning the language, I rewrote that manuscript, this time in Italian, but with the same content and the same title, which is taken from a poem by the wonderful Jószef Attila. My first book came out in Italy in 1959. Today I am the Vice President of the Società Dante Alighieri* and I speak and write a lot about language issues. Language for me is everything. Much more important than the

---

*Founded in 1889 with the objective of promoting the Italian language throughout the world.

idea of homeland. All I am, all I have done is thanks to the Italian language, which I find to be airy, it is a language that breaths between letters, a language that comes naturally. When I write a poem in Italian, the language pulls me forward, one word pulls the next, and together they move forward. I think that it is a language well suited for writing, for poetry and for songs. It is a beautiful language because it is musical.

GR You have been writing for more than sixty years and produced more than twenty volumes of prose and poetry in the Italian language. How would you say that your writings have changed over the years? How would you describe your writing career?

EB I hope that there has been an evolution in my writings, even when I return to the same themes. But there will never be enough writing about Auschwitz. One can never say it all, even with a hundred or a thousand books. I think that what Alberto Moravia used to tell me, that all books are to some extent autobiographical, is true and that a writer always writes what he or she has lived, seen, experienced. I believe that a writer is always a witness to her times. In my writings there are also a lot of references to events happening today. Because unfortunately what we see today is a growing fascism, racism, and anti-Semitism. There are moments when it is important to speak up and make the changes, however small they might be, that one person can make.

GR Who are the writers you admire and love reading?

EB It's better perhaps to read than to know some writers. For me the character and the human profile of a person are very important. I met all the great Italian writers. I loved the poet Eugenio Montale and the writer Vasco Pratolini, who became a friend. In writers, I mainly look for their human qualities. For me, they may have won the Nobel Prize, but if they have no human value, I am not interested in them. I also love American literature: Saul Bellow, Isaac Bashevis Singer, Henry Roth, Philip Roth, Ernest Hemingway. I knew Moravia well, I met Bassani. I just wrote a preface for an exhibit on Bassani, of whom I actually was not terribly fond. And Primo Levi, of course. A dear friend since the 1970s until his death. Two days before he died, he called me. I was the one trying to console him, as if I were the older and not the younger among us. We saw each other often.

GR How did the two of you meet? Can you share a specific memory of your friendship with him?

EB There are many such memories. One, for instance: Primo and his wife were my guests and we were having lunch at my house. It was me, my husband Nelo, and them. We looked at each other eating. Nelo was poking around with his chicken, leaving some meat on the bone. Primo's wife was doing the same. Primo and I cleaned up the plate until the last crumb of bread. It was enough to see ourselves eating to understand what we had gone through. Nelo and Primo's wife could not understand, because they did not experience what we did. As for another memory:

it was typical of Primo to carefully observe his surroundings. He was an observer in the camps as well, when he scrutinized the surroundings from within and without the experience he was living. He was able to walk around my small living room for an hour and look carefully at the table for twenty minutes. I would say to him: What are you looking at? And he would quietly look at the table for twenty minutes. It was his nature. As for when we met, Primo and I have different versions. We met in the middle of the '60s when he came to visit me while they were shooting a film in Turin based on my short story "Silvia." He appeared on the set in Via Verdi and looked like Alice in Wonderland: he had never seen a film set, I think, and he was struck by the lights, the costumes. I think he was a little bit in love with Cinema. This is my memory of our first encounter. According to Primo, instead, we met in Cuneo, when Nelo was shooting his film *La strada più lunga*, and Primo and I met in a café where we got a little tipsy and I gave him a rose. Instead, he was the one who brought me a rose when he came to Via Verdi to see the shooting of the film. It is wonderful, I think, that we both have our own version of when we met for the first time.

GR You often say that you and Primo Levi were "brother and sister of the lager." To what extent did Auschwitz define your friendship as adults and writers in Italy?

EB We were close but also different. Let's not forget that he was a Jewish man of the Italian bourgeoisie and I was a poor Jewish girl from rural Hungary when we arrived in Auschwitz. In a certain sense, I was spared some of the moral suffering Primo went through. Not because I did not understand what was going on, but the harshness of the situation affected me less inside. Primo suffered morally more than me. He was already a formed man with a university degree and a civil consciousness that I did not have yet. After we met, we always sent each other our publications, we met often, and sometimes he would ask me questions about the Yiddish culture, of which he knew very little. His death left me orphaned as a Holocaust survivor, I still feel the void of his absence as a writer and a friend.

GR On February 20th of 2021, Pope Francis came to visit you in your home. You have spoken publicly of the symbolic and human meaning of this visit. Can you describe the meeting?

EB The first time I met him, Pope Francis came to my home. I thought it was remarkable that he would want to come here. After ten minutes the whole world knew about it. I received calls from everywhere, the United States, Argentina, Brazil. His visit meant a lot to me, because when he expressed the desire to meet me, after reading my "Letter to God" and an interview I gave a journalist of the *Osservatore Romano*, he decided that he was going to visit me at my home. He did not want me to go to him. Before he came, I had heard that he approved of my letter. I was not sure what he meant by that. When he entered the house,

I was very moved and began to cry. He told me to breathe deeply and then opened his arms. I am also a person who likes to embrace. Everybody says that two humanities met that day. He stayed a couple of hours and I asked him what he meant by saying that he approved of my letter, and he whispered that God is a constant search. Then he gave me a copy of his encyclical with a dedication in which he thanked me for all I do, especially with young people. It is a beautiful dedication, but what I like the most about it is that his signature is written all in tiny letters and it simply says Francesco. He also apologized to the victims of the Shoah as he did during his visit at the Yad Vashem in Jerusalem. After that I met him again in the Vatican on January 27th of 2022, for International Holocaust Remembrance Day. We spoke of our aching knees, he gave me a cashmere shawl which he put on my shoulders (I thought I was wearing a tallit), and I brought him challah. The next day I received an album with beautiful pictures taken during our meeting.

Rome, Summer 2022

Edith Bruck was born in Hungary in 1931, and as a young teen she was deported with her family to the concentration camps of Auschwitz, Dachau, Christianstadt, Landsberg, and Bergen-Belsen, where she lost both her parents and a brother. After the end of WWII, she briefly returned to Hungary, lived in Czechoslovakia, and then moved to Israel, where she stayed for three years. Working for a dancing troupe in 1954 she traveled to Italy where she decided to settle and where she still lives today.

Bruck is the author of more than twenty books, both prose and poetry, devoted to her life-long commitment to Holocaust testimony, starting with *Who Loves You Like This* (1959 in Italian and 2000 in English, published by Paul Dry Books). She has won several Italian literary awards; most recently, in 2021, *Lost Bread* was a finalist for the prestigious *Premio Strega* and winner of *Premio Strega giovani* (youth).

Bruck has gained national and international recognition for her writings in Holocaust testimony and, more generally, in contemporary Italian literature.

Among other honors, in 2021 she received the *Cavalieriato di Gran Croce*, conferred by the President of Italy. Along with Primo Levi, Edith Bruck is one of the most prolific writers of Holocaust narratives in Italian. Her books have been translated into many languages including English, French, German, Dutch, Polish, Hungarian, and Hebrew. She lives in Rome.

Gabriella Romani is Professor of Italian at Seton Hall University. With Brenda Webster she translated Edith Bruck's *Letter to My Mother* (2006) and Enrico Castelnuovo's *The Moncalvos* (2017). She is from Rome and now lives in Philadelphia.

David Yanoff is an attorney and author from Philadelphia.